Alone

His room was gone. He was on a bare rocky hillside, brown and harsh under a wintry sky. He lifted his eyes, astounded, and saw mountains all around; a vast ring of mountains, sharp and bleak, with slashes of snow in the ravines. He could see black birds circling the peaks, and in the wind their cries carried to him, solitary and wild. . . .

Other Scholastic books
you will enjoy:

Herb Seasoning
by Julian Thompson

Storm Rising
by Marilyn Singer

The Changeover
by Margaret Mahy

After the Bomb
by Gloria Miklowitz

point

A TIME OF DARKNESS

Sherryl Jordan

SCHOLASTIC INC.
New York Toronto London Auckland Sydney

ISBN 0-590-43362-8

12 11 10 9 8 7 6 5 4 3 2 1   3   2 3 4 5 6 7/9

Printed in the U.S.A.   01

My deepest thanks to
Andreas Vollenweider
whose music "White Winds"
inspired the Valley of Anshur,
and became a part of the whole
amazing and joyous experience
that was the writing
of this novel.

A TIME
OF DARKNESS

One

The wind hissed and sighed in the crevices of the cave, tore the fire into shreds and spun the embers, spitting sparks, into the smoky dark. On a pile of glimmering straw, buried in furs, a youth lay in troubled sleep. There was a movement outside the cave; a sound of stone grating on stone, and a blackness passed before the cave's mouth. Yellow eyes burned a moment in the firelight, and the shadow passed.

The youth woke, tossed aside the heavy furs, and rolled onto his knees. He was naked. He groped in the leaping shadows for a blanket, dragged it around him, and stumbled over to the fire. Crouching, he picked up a long bone from the cave floor, prodded the charred outer logs into the fire's heart, and sniffed noisily. A battered black metal pot was suspended from sticks above the fire, and he stirred its contents with the bone. The smell of stewed meat, onions, and herbs mingled with the thick smoke.

He got up again and went over to a low bench carved deep into the wall of the cave. Crude pottery bowls were piled there in tidy heaps; spoons carved from bone, and several handmade knives with thick bone handles. He drew the coarse blanket closer, held the edges together in his teeth, and picked up a spoon and a cracked bowl. With a corner of the blanket he wiped the gritty dust out of the bowl, returned to the fire, and ladled out some of the stew. Again, he crouched on the floor. With the spoon halfway to his mouth he paused, listening. His eyes, half hidden under tangled black curls, flickered green and gold in the flames. His nose, straight and slightly hooked, gave him a look of superiority, almost of arrogance. But his mouth opened slightly in alarm, and he panted suddenly like an animal, wary and afraid.

Soundlessly, he put the bowl and spoon on the rough earth beside him, gathered up the blanket, and stood. He listened a long time, tense.

"Ayoshe?" he called hoarsely, but his voice was drowned in the howling wind outside. Slowly, he walked around the fire and stood in the cave entrance. The sky was silver-blue with stars, and the wind thrashed hard and raw across his face. Uneasily, he pulled the blanket closer about him. He remembered he should have brought a stick with him, or a spear. Would he never learn? For a while he stood motionless, listening. He shivered, swore under his breath, and turned back to the cave. Then he saw it.

A wolf, mangy and thin, was watching him. He froze. The wolf too was still, its yellow eyes fixed on his face. It walked into the cave, growling, the fur raised along its spine. It sniffed the hearth and the furs of the bed. It seemed to know the place, and to be disturbed to find a stranger here. It turned towards the youth, and he backed away out onto the ledge. The wolf followed, forcing him further from the cave, further out along the crumbling windswept ledge that was all he had between the sheer cliff wall and the precipice. Glancing down, he saw rough rocks jutting out five meters below. Beyond them, tumbling away in the bright night, silver-edged and stark, were crumbling cliffs, overhanging rocks, and steep ravines. Far below was the desert, silent and smooth under the howling wind.

He glanced back at the wolf, and took a step towards the cave. The animal bared its teeth and sprang. He felt the impact of its body, coarse and hard and warm. He smelled its breath and felt smooth teeth and saliva like slime across his cheek. The stars spun, and he knew he was falling. He screamed.

He woke then, bolt upright, shaking, and wet with sweat. The wolf's head glared from the greyness of his bedroom wall, then faded. He felt the bed with his hands. He touched cotton sheets, cool and smooth. He collapsed back on his pillow, and wiped his face on his pajama sleeve. Saliva glistened on the material, and the right side of his face stung. The room was full of smoke, and he could still smell stew. He lay with his hands over his face, his throat dry and sore, his right shoulder and back throbbing with pain.

"Rocco?" His bedroom door opened, and his father, Harlan Makepeace, came in. Light from

3

the passage poured into the room, gold and comforting across the clothes strewn on the floor, the homework spread unfinished across his desk, his stereo and books and old model planes. His father sat on the bed, frowning. He looked younger in the half light, gentle and boyish.

"Are you all right, Rocco?" he asked anxiously. "You called out."

"I'm fine," Rocco lied, wondering whether his shoulder was broken, and wishing the smoke would stop stinging his eyes. "I can't breathe, that's all."

"I think you'd better see a doctor. This has gone on for almost two weeks now."

"It's only that dream. It keeps coming back."

"About the wolf?"

"It's pretty real, Dad." Rocco swallowed loudly, and attempted a smile. His right cheek felt as if it had been skinned.

"Is something worrying you?" asked his father gently. "Your exams, maybe?"

"No. Everything's fine."

"Are you sure?"

"Positive. Dad, is there anything wrong with my face? Is it bleeding, or cut, or anything?"

"Looks the same as usual to me. You're a bit white, that's all. Maybe you're sickening for something. Try to get some more sleep. It's only two o'clock."

Just before his father closed the door, Rocco asked: "Dad? Do you smell anything?"

"Only your socks. Time you put them in the wash."

"Not that. Smoke."

"No, can't say I do. Maybe someone was burning rubbish last night, and the smoke came in your window. It's gone now. Try to sleep."

His door clicked shut, and Rocco sat up and switched on the light above his bed. He sniffed his hands, rubbed them through his hair, and sniffed his palms. The smell of smoke was strong on his skin, and particles of grit fell out of his hair onto the white sheet. He touched them, puzzled and shocked. He'd washed his hair last night in the shower, just before he came to bed. He fingered his cheek carefully. It felt perfectly normal to touch, yet was as sore as if he had grazed off half the skin. He sniffed his hands again, frowning. Next time he'd rub ashes all over his face, and use one of those knives to give himself a haircut. Maybe his father would notice that.

Rocco's young sister, Amber, listened eagerly to the conversation at breakfast. "If Rocco is sick," she said hopefully, her mouth full of toast, "and if he dies, can I have his stereo?"

"I'm not sick," Rocco said irritably. "Just tired. Anyway, if I croak, my stereo goes to Brent."

"That's not fair," Amber sulked. "And your eyes are all red. You've been crying."

"I have not. I've been sitting in smoke all night."

"You're getting the flu," said his mother, as she dug in her bag for the car keys. "Your voice is hoarse, too. You've got one of those viruses going around. You'd better not be sick for your exams. Where are my keys?"

"In the fruit bowl," said Harlan, into his coffee

mug. "Where you threw them last night."

Rocco's mother collected the keys, checked her smooth hair and lipstick in the dining room mirror, and shot her husband a meaningful look. "We'll finish that discussion when I get home," she said.

"There's nothing more to discuss," he replied calmly. "She's arriving Friday, and that's all there is to it."

"She's not staying a week, though."

"No. A month." He gave her a disarming smile. "You'd better go, Stephanie, if you don't want to get caught in the rush traffic. See you tonight."

"If you're lucky," she said, and left.

"Is Aunty Simone coming again?" asked Amber, pleased.

"She's arriving Friday night," said her father. He glanced at his watch. "You'd better hurry, Rocco. You've got your lunch to make, yet. And put your dirty washing out. I'm not going into your room again, while it's in its present state. If you run out of clean clothes, that's your problem."

"Suits me," said Rocco.

Amber giggled. "You'll look funny biking to school with no clothes on," she said.

"I wouldn't bike, I'd walk," said Rocco, "and people would have more time to admire me."

"I mean it, Rocco," said his father, standing up and beginning to clear the table. "It's no wonder you dream about animals. I picked up a yogurt carton from under your bed yesterday, and a family of cockroaches crawled out. I should get dirt money for doing your room. I wouldn't sleep in it for anything."

"I'll clean it up after school," said Rocco, going over to the bench and beginning to make sandwiches.

"You're seeing your grandmother on the way home, remember," his father said. "She's expecting you. Don't disappoint her."

Rocco sighed, cut his finger slicing a tomato, and swore quietly. "She's old, Dad. I don't know what to talk to her about. And she's always going on about Russia, and Doctor Daley, and the food, and the stupid nurses."

"It doesn't matter what you talk about," said Harlan. "Just taking the time to visit her is enough. Talk about anything. School, your archery club, anything."

"She doesn't listen. She gets everything mixed up. She calls me Alex sometimes."

"She's senile, Rocco. She can't help it. And you do look like Alex. Very like him, actually."

"But he's been dead for seven years, Dad!"

"Not dead. Missing. There's a slight difference."

"Mum says he's in prison," piped up Amber, shoving Rocco aside and aiming detergent roughly in the direction of the sink.

"Watch it! You've got soap all over my sandwiches!" Rocco yelled.

"I'll wash, young lady, you dry," said their father, wedging himself between them. "If your lunch is ruined, Rocco, buy one. And your Uncle Alex isn't in prison. He just disappeared. Nobody knows where he went."

"I bet he went down in a plane somewhere," said Rocco, taking some money from a pottery bowl in a cupboard, and slinging his schoolbag over his shoulder. He winced, and changed the bag to the other side. "He'll be dead, Dad. Nobody disappears for seven years and stays alive and never contacts anyone again."

"I think he murdered someone," said Amber, stroking the tea towel tenderly along the bread knife. "He murdered them, and went away to hide."

"Maybe he was the one who got murdered," said Rocco. "See you later, Dad."

As he went out into the warm, bright sun, Rocco stepped through a stinging wave of acrid smoke. It was thick with the smell of stew, onions, and herbs. He glanced over the fence to see if the neighbor's incinerator was going. It was not. There was no smoke anywhere. He sighed heavily, and got his bike out of the garage. His back was sore, he could hardly move his shoulder, and his whole body ached as if it had been pummeled. Wearily, he biked to school.

His grandmother was asleep when he arrived that afternoon, and he was tempted to leave without speaking to her. The ward smelled of flowers, talcum powder, antiseptic, and wet beds. While he waited for her to wake up, Rocco examined the array of family photographs on her locker. There was a photo of himself and Amber, taken at a Christmas party two years ago. He had been fourteen then, and she had been seven. There was his parents' wedding photo, with his mother looking plump, curly-haired and laughing. His dad had never changed. He'd always been boyish and thin, roughly good-looking, with straight black hair. Rocco looked like neither of them. He looked like Uncle Alex there, pale-eyed and solemn in his pilot's uniform. His nose was too big as well.

There was a rustle in the bed, and Rocco's grandmother stirred. She looked pink and bothered, embarrassed to have been caught asleep.

"Oh — I am sorry, Alex," she murmured, struggling to sit up, pulling her pink bed jacket closer around her shoulders. "I was just having a little nap. I didn't sleep well, last night. Crazy dreams. How are you, dear? You don't look quite your usual self. Had an accident, have you?"

"I'm fine. I'm Rocco, Grandma. Not Alex."

"Yes, I know. Sit down dear, here, on the bed." She took his hand and held on to it, and he glanced warily around the ward. Only the old people saw, peering like inquisitive birds from the white pillows, wondering.

"Well, tell me what you've been up to," said his grandmother brightly. "Still playing the drums?"

"No. That's Amber, not me. I go to archery. I've just bought a new sight for my bow. It's great, magnifies the target." He tried to withdraw his hand, but she held it in a vicelike grip, patted it with her free hand, and rubbed his wrist. Her hands were large and soft, and she smelled of talcum powder.

"Have you still got all those model planes your Uncle Alex gave you, when he joined the Air Force?" she asked.

He nodded. "They're in perfect condition still.

9

And all the books about aeronautics, and the photos of the jets he took on test flights."

"I'm glad, dear. He made those, with his own hands. He threw the birds' eggs away. That's what got him into flying, though. When he was your age, he had the highest respect for birds."

"Why?"

"Because they could fly, and he couldn't. Here's the nurse with the tea trolly. Will you get my tea? Milk, with two sugars. None of those little white pills."

She released his hand, and he jumped up. The nurse smiled as she handed him a cup of tea. "Your gran's a bit better today, isn't she?" she murmured. "Quite rational. Has she given you any letters to post?"

Rocco looked surprised. "She's not still writing them, is she?"

"She never gives up," smiled the nurse. "If she gives you one, just throw it away as usual."

Rocco hesitated, toying with the spoon on the saucer. "What if they really are important?" he asked.

The nurse's smile widened. "She's senile, Rocco. All the letters are to Russia. We opened one, once. It was only a few lines. It didn't make any sense at all. She was asking someone to bring her back some dust from Mars."

Rocco shrugged, and took the tea back to his grandmother. When she was safely sipping, he sat on the edge of the stool at the foot of her bed.

"I've got to go soon, Grandma," he said. "I've got a stack of homework. Exams are in a week.

And Dad says I've got to tidy my room."

"Harlan works hard to look after your home," murmured the old lady. "I think your mother bosses him."

Rocco grinned. "Dad enjoys it. And being home all day gives him time for his pottery and things."

His grandmother was silent, sipping her tea. Through the steam her eyes watched him, narrowed, very black, and uncomfortably shrewd. He looked away and made some comment about the weather.

"You could be proud of your father, Rocco," she said gently. "He's a special human being, in many ways. I don't think you fully appreciate your family."

"I've really got to go, Grandma," he muttered, standing up. He made the mistake of meeting her eyes.

"You can't fight it, Rocco," she said.

"I'm not fighting anything. I just wish Dad was ordinary, that's all. No one else's father stays home all day and does the washing and makes garden gnomes."

"But he's not ordinary, Rocco. He's got . . . well, he inherited it from me. He and Simone, both. It's in their blood. And yours."

Rocco pushed his chin out, and glared at her. "If you're talking about their mental telepathy and all that, you're wrong," he said hotly. "They're weird, that's all. And none of that stuff is true, anyway. Scientists have explained it all. It's not special. It's coincidence and guesswork, and good luck."

"Careful, young man. You'll end up like your mother."

"What's that supposed to mean?"

"No sense of humor, Rocco. She fights it, all the way. She's too logical. That's why she's a good lawyer, I suppose. But it's spoiled her for our family. She can't stand Simone, and look at all the fun she misses."

"It isn't always fun. Last time Simone stayed, she and Dad got drunk and smashed Mum's Spanish lady. It cost over six hundred dollars."

"That was an accident. And it was an ugly thing, anyway."

"Ugly? That was ugly? What about all Dad's revolting little gnomes? They're not even human. They're deformities. He doesn't even paint them, just leaves them looking like bandy-legged goblins with moss and stuff growing all over them. One's got toadstools hanging out its nose, and he think it's funny. He's got them all over the garden, weathering, he says. I can't take my friends home because they'll find out."

His grandmother finished her tea and put the cup and saucer on the locker, between the photographs.

"I won't argue with you, Alex," she sighed, closing her eyes. "We've argued too many times. You always were a misfit, the black sheep of the family."

"Rocco. I'm Rocco, not Alex!"

She opened her eyes again. "Don't shout. I'm not deaf."

"Sorry, Grandma. I'm going now. I'll come and see you again after the exams."

"Rocco? Will you look in that top drawer of

my locker? There's a letter there, and some money for stamps."

He sighed, and pulled open the drawer. He left the money, but picked up the letter. It was a thin blue aerogramme. The writing was small, but tidy. "Alexei Bibikov," he read. The address was a city called Baikonur, in Russia. He glanced at his grandmother. She was watching his face.

"Please post it," she said. "I've had it five weeks, waiting until you came. The nurses throw them away." She looked so helpless, so pleading and earnest, he smiled. He folded the letter in half and placed it carefully in his shirt pocket.

"Of course I will, Grandma."

"Promise me, Rocco."

He hesitated. "I promise."

She lay back on the pillows, and he thought she had fallen asleep. He bent down as if to kiss her forehead, changed his mind, and stood up again. She opened her eyes.

"You've been smoking at school," she said. "It's bad for you."

"I haven't."

"Don't lie, Rocco. I might be crazy, but I'm not stupid. Your hair reeks of smoke."

He drew back, startled. She gave him a half smile, and winked. "Never mind, I won't tell. And when you get home, ask your father to put something on your face. That's a nasty graze. I suppose you were showing off on your bike, and came a cropper. Well, don't stand staring like that. I'm not one of your father's gnomes. Off you go, and don't forget to post my letter."

TWO

Rocco biked home slowly, avoiding the main streets. He was aching all over again, and felt as if all the energy had been drained out of him. His brain felt like scrambled eggs. He blamed his grandmother for that. He'd been all right, until she'd talked about smoke and something being wrong with his face.

At a street corner he stopped by a post office and took the aerogramme out of his pocket. He spread it flat, and read the address again. He tried to open the letter without tearing it, but couldn't.

"Stupid old cow," he said angrily, and screwed the letter into a ball. He aimed it expertly at a nearby rubbish bin, and rode painfully home.

He collapsed face down on his unmade bed, and for ten minutes lay without moving. Then he groaned, sighed heavily, got up, and changed into his jeans and a purple shirt. He checked his jeans pocket for money, went out again, got on his bike, and went back to the rubbish bin. He leaned over it, resting his elbows on the rim, and slowly sifted through the garbage. He ignored the glances and comments of people walking by. He was too tired to care. He found the letter and stood up. He smoothed the blue paper flat, wiped the tomato sauce off it, and got on his bike again.

He was the last customer at the post office. The man behind the counter looked dubiously at the orange-stained envelope, shot Rocco a suspicious look, and pushed the stamps across the counter. Rocco posted the letter and went home.

His father was in the kitchen, peeling vegetables.

"Hi, Rocco. How did your day go? Did you remember to see your grandmother?"

Rocco nodded over his glass of ginger beer.

"How was she?"

"Same as usual. Called me Alex, and we talked about planes, smoking, and birds."

Harlan grinned. "Any letters to post today?"

"Nope." Rocco wiped his mouth on his sleeve, and placed the glass in the sink.

"Tallulah phoned," said his father. "She wants you to go swimming with her. Are you all right? You look awful."

"You look at gnomes all day, and say I look bad? Thanks."

"You're welcome. You'd better phone her back. She's waiting."

"I'll see her tomorrow. I'm going to bed."

Harlan's eyebrows rose, but he made no comment.

As he passed the dining table, Rocco's eyes

fell on a drawing his father had done. He stopped, astounded. The drawing was of a cave, strikingly similar to the cave in his dream. He picked up the drawing, and shot his father an uneasy look. "What's this?" he asked, trying to sound non-chalant.

"It's a design for an entry in the pottery competition next year," Harlan replied, picking up another potato, and starting to peel it. "I'm making a cave with a family of trolls." He glanced at Rocco's face, and grinned. "Well, you don't have to look so alarmed. That's only the first sketch. The finished thing'll be better."

Rocco licked his dry lips, and tried to smile. "It's terrific, Dad."

"I'm going to light their fire electrically, so it's glowing," went on Harlan. "And I'll cut up that old fox fur of your grandmother's to make them a fur bed. Thought I'd make some little bowls and things on shelves, too."

Rocco dropped the drawing on the table as if it were a hot coal. "Sounds great," he muttered.

"Thanks. Your mother thinks I'm mad. Says I ought to make something useful, for a change. Like a casserole dish, or coffee mugs. She's got no idea about inspiration, or the power of the imagination. She thinks fantasy's a waste of time. She'll learn, when my trolls carry off first prize and a trip for two to Rome. Reckon you and I could have a great time, there."

Rocco leaned against the edge of the table, and studied his father's profile. "Why did you marry Mum?" he asked suddenly.

Harlan rinsed the peeled potatoes, put them

in a saucepan of water, and placed them on the stove. He shrugged and started making a salad. "Loved her, I suppose," he said.

Rocco was too tired to decide whether that was funny or tragic. "You've got absolutely nothing in common," he murmured.

"Yes we have," said Harlan. "We both enjoy spending her money. Besides, she's good for me. Necessary. She keeps my feet on the ground, planted firmly in reality."

Rocco grinned. "If you design troll caves when you're in reality, I dread to think what you'd come up with in an artistic frenzy."

"I dread it myself," said Harlan. "Could be worse than your wolf." He looked at Rocco's face, and sighed, "Why don't you lie down, son, before you fall down? You can study later, when you're refreshed."

Rocco nodded wearily and left. Frowning, his father watched him go, then he went and picked up the phone.

In his room Rocco pulled off his sneakers and socks, opened his window, and drew his curtains against the bright afternoon sun. A gust of wind flung back the curtain and whispered past his face, bringing with it a breath of woodsmoke, vegetables, and herbs. He pushed aside the curtain and leaned out, sniffing. The wind blew steady and strong, lifting his hair and cooling the hot graze on his cheek. He put his hand to his face, and when he looked at his fingers they were smeared with blood. He rushed to the mirror and saw what his grandmother had seen.

The graze was livid, ingrained with dust and

tiny stones, and weeping fluid and blood. He tore off his shirt and looked over his shoulder at his back. It was mottled with bruises, and his right shoulder was raw. He put on his shirt, carefully buttoned it up, tucked it into his jeans, and looked at himself severely in the mirror.

"You've got a terrific imagination, Rocco," he said solemnly. "There's really nothing wrong with you. Nothing. Nothing. Nothing."

He stood beside his bed, braced himself, and dropped backwards onto the crumpled sheets and blankets. He gave a howl of agony.

Harlan opened the door and stood at the foot of the bed, looking alarmed. "I heard you call out," he said. "What's wrong?"

"Nothing," croaked Rocco, too agonized to move. "Nothing that a spell in a loony bin wouldn't fix."

"What do you mean?"

"Can't you see my face?"

"Yes. It's where it usually is."

"I'm serious, Dad. Half my face is skinned alive. I fell down a cliff last night, when the wolf attacked me. I've been in agony all day. My back's black and blue. I'm lucky I wasn't killed."

For a while Harlan studied his face sympathetically. "Are you sure you haven't got anything you want to talk about?" he asked gently. "No problems? Drugs? Anything like that? I won't be angry if you have been trying them, Rocco. I know a lot of your friends do. But I will be angry if you lie about it."

"I haven't taken anything, Dad. Honest. It's just my dream. Sometimes I think it's not a dream at all, it's something else. But it's not drugs. Not unless it's something in the herbs."

"Herbs? What herbs?"

"In the stew. But I don't think I ate any. The wolf came before I had a chance."

For a while his father was silent. Then he said, "I think it's time you talked to someone. I've made us an appointment to see the doctor this evening. Seven-thirty."

"What's going on, Dad? Am I crazy?"

"Of course not, Rocco. You're deeply disturbed about something. Maybe you're hallucinating. Maybe what your mother said was right; maybe you do have a virus, and it's causing fever, visual disturbances, and altering the way you feel things. I don't know. We'll find out in a few hours. Try to get some rest. I'll wake you up in time for your appointment."

He went out again and Rocco lay perfectly still, his back smarting where a fold of blanket bit into raw flesh. He suddenly felt desperately tired, weak, and at the end of his endurance. He wanted to sleep, yet he was afraid of his dream. He wanted to switch off his brain, to rest awhile without thinking, without feeling.

A sudden gust threw aside his curtain and burst in like a small whirlwind, bringing with it sand and dirt. His room reeked of smoke. He closed his eyes and let the wind blow over him. He tasted grit in his mouth, and felt dust pricking his eyelids. The wind sighed and moaned, and he thought he heard voices in it, rising and falling, sometimes in song, sometimes in strange piercing wails. The sounds became confused, mingled with the tumult of the wind, and died away.

Out of the stillness came a child's voice, singing. It was a lilting, happy song, clear and sweet, and all his senses were drawn to it, and warmed. He heard his curtain move, and a door bang somewhere in the house. Amber's transistor radio went on, and the music played faintly in the distance. Still the child's voice sang, pure and sweet and strong, and Rocco sighed deeply and smiled. If this was madness, he welcomed it. He welcomed too the coolness of the wind and the sudden clarity of thought that came with it. His pain diminished. He felt as if all his world was slipping quietly sideways, and another dimension was sliding alongside, crystal clear and compelling. Time seemed suspended. Excitement built in him, and he hardly breathed, savoring the sensations. He felt intensely aware and alive, yet deeply at peace. The other dimension slid closer, converging with his world somewhere just behind his eyes, and he opened his mind and accepted it.

For a while he seemed to float. His body became numb, and deathly cold. He felt a movement on his face, and realized that pieces of sand and grit were being blown across his skin. The wind whistled in like ice, bitterly cold, and somewhere a bell chimed. He rolled over, fumbling for the blankets, and the grit slid down his face and clattered onto his bed. The pillow bit into his face like a rock. His eyes stung, and gritty soil ground between his teeth. His bed was full of rubble, and the gale whipped his face with dust. Blindly he scrambled up, wiping his streaming eyes on his sleeve.

His room was gone. He was on a bare rocky hillside, brown and harsh under a wintry sky. He lifted his eyes, astounded, and saw mountains all around; a vast ring of mountains, sharp and bleak, with slashes of snow in the ravines. He could see black birds circling the peaks, and in the wind their cries carried to him, solitary and wild.

In the center of the ranges was a valley. A river ran through it, beginning in the lonely mountains on Rocco's left, and bubbling on down through the flat dusty plain of the valley floor. It vanished into the ranges opposite, rushing out in turbulent rapids through savage ravines and black, sunless cliffs. On Rocco's side of the river, slightly to his left, was a small forest of spruce trees. The tall green spires were the only rich color in the valley.

Directly below him, where the river ran shallow and slow, was a primitive rope bridge. Rocco looked beyond the bridge, across a stretch of bare and dusty earth, and on up to a high cliff. He stared, amazed.

The cliff was terraced into wide ledges on different levels, and at the back of each ledge was a cave. Paths connected the caves; crooked tracks cut into the cliff face itself, and running up and down between the levels, sometimes broken and spanned by rickety wooden planks, and sometimes cut into rough stairs. Where the track was steep or there were narrow wooden planks, there were crude handrails made of rope or strips of hide.

The caves were of different sizes. Flaps of ragged animal skins covered the entrances, and hanging in the dark spaces above were odd cylinders of varying lengths, sometimes flashing like metal. Some of the caves had fires in them, and Rocco could see smoke crawling out around the edges of the skins, and puffing in tattered clouds from the spaces above.

Sounds came from the dwellings; the hollow-sounding laughter of children at play within the caves, a girl's voice calling, and a dull thudding sound, like someone pounding grain. He could smell smoke from the cave fires, and meat and vegetables cooking. The wind whipped along the cliff face, scattering smoke and tossing the skins in the cave entrances, moving the strange metallic shapes hanging in the spaces above. There was a rich, beautiful ringing sound like bells, and Rocco realized that the hanging shapes were wind chimes.

To the left of the cave dwellings, where the cliff broke up into jagged mountain rock, there was a garden surrounded by a stone wall. A few people worked there, sowing seeds across the ploughed earth. At one end of the garden were several rows of leafy vegetables. A boy was kneeling between the rows, weeding.

The valley floor and lower mountain slopes were sparsely covered with tough tussock grass, growing in clumps between the rocks. The land was bronzed and tranquil, with a wild, bleak beauty that appealed to Rocco. He shivered, rubbed his hands on his frozen arms, and began the descent. He made his way towards the bridge, stumbling on the sharp rocks, wishing he'd left on his shoes. Lower down, the slopes were sheltered from the bitter wind. The ground became more level, and was warmed by the sun.

He had almost reached the bridge when he noticed, between the rocks and tussock grass, something white. He bent to pick it up. It was a bone, long, and weathered smooth and white. Nearby lay several others, smaller and broken. He saw another bone, large and domed, perfect, with fine zigzag joins. He rolled it over with his foot and it clattered away on the stones, grinning. He cried out, and someone laughed.

A solitary child was squatting on the stones, watching him. She was five or six, fair-haired and blue-eyed, and wearing a thick shapeless dress that looked as if it had been woven and sewn by hand. There were only gaping holes for sleeves, and her arms were thin and blue with cold.

Rocco stared at her for a few moments, then he slowly smiled and crouched in front of her. "Hello," he said. "What's your name?"

"Tisha."

She smiled shyly and moved her right hand over the ground between them. She collected up five small bones and bunched them in her palm. She was playing knucklebones, with real knuckles. For a while Rocco watched, saying nothing. She continued her game, glancing curiously every now and again through her tangled hair, to look at his face. She began singing, and it was the lilting, happy tune he had heard before. Her long hair moved in the mountain wind, and smelled of herbs and smoke.

After a while he said, "What are you doing out here, Tisha?"

"Playing," she said. "They won't look after me."

"Who won't? Your parents?" He picked one of the bones out of her small dirty hand, and examined it.

"They be dead and burned," she said, taking the knuckle back. "Imma and the others, they won't." Her accent was strange, and some words she emphasized in odd places, but Rocco had no difficulty understanding her. He watched her, fascinated.

The cloth of her garment was different from anything he had ever seen. It wasn't woven from cotton or wool. Goathair, maybe. There was something earthy and primitive about her, and about the whole place that intrigued and appealed to him.

While he studied Tisha, she studied him. She fingered the buttons on his shirt, his clean fingernails, and stared in wonder at the changing digits on his watch. She leaned forward to see it better, and he noticed fragments of straw in her tousled hair. She rubbed his shirt sleeve, frowning.

"What is it?" she asked.

"A shirt."

"That I know! What color?"

"Purple."

"Pur-ple." She repeated the word several times, slowly, and a wide smile broke across her face. "I like purple," she said. Then suddenly serious she asked: "What did you bring?"

"Bring? I didn't bring anything."

She laughed, and nodded. "Yes, you did. You have to."

"What do I have to bring?"

She shrugged. "Anything. Clothes, arrowheads, weaving, dried fish." She leaned forward again and stared closely into his face. "You be not sick?" she asked seriously. "Petur won't let you in, if you be sick."

"No . . . I don't think I'm ill. Why?"

Her eyes slid past his shoulder, and she stood up, her pale face reddening. Rocco also stood and turned around.

A group of children were gathered behind him, their faces hard and hostile. They stared at him, saying nothing. Rocco glanced down at Tisha, but she edged away from him and went to stand near the tallest girl, who looked several years younger than Rocco, and very grim. The girl grabbed Tisha's arm and pushed her roughly behind her.

With growing uneasiness, Rocco waited for one of them to speak. They were dressed as Tisha was, in shapeless, homemade garments. Some wore belts of twisted hide, leather trousers and jerkins, or jackets made of fur. All the seams were stitched with fine leather strips. Several of the older children wore handmade boots of animal skin, bound tightly to their legs with leather cords. Rocco could see pieces of fur poking out around the tops. His own feet ached on the cold stones, and he felt foreign and uncomfortable in his rich-colored shirt and well-cut jeans. He was an intruder in their world, alien and awkward.

"Where is your place?" asked one of the older

boys. He was about ten, and was wiry and tough. He carried a leather quiver of arrows across his back, and held a large wooden bow. Another boy gripped a heavy stick, rounded and stained darkly at one end. A dead rabbit, its head crushed, hung on a rough rope from his waist.

"My place?" repeated Rocco. "It's — it's a city, a long way from here."

"Where's your cart?" asked the boy with the rabbit.

"I didn't bring one."

"You be no trader, then?"

Rocco shook his head. The boy glanced at the older girl, and she frowned slightly and shook her head. She studied Rocco's face, her blue eyes narrowed and suspicious. "If you be come from beyond The Voidances," she said, "what have you eaten all the days? Where be your blankets, your weapons?"

"I haven't got any," said Rocco. He smiled and added lightly, "I left in a hurry. I didn't have time to pack."

An alarmed murmur ran through the group, and the girl shouted at them to be quiet, and to move back. They moved away, and the older ones stood between Rocco and the younger ones, protectively.

Rocco's smile faded, and his sense of unease increased. The girl who seemed to be in charge watched him closely, her eyes crawling over his hair, his clothes, his skin. He guessed she was the leader, Imma, of whom Tisha had spoken. "Do you be ill?" she asked suddenly.

"I'm fine, I think," Rocco replied. "I'd feel

better if you didn't look at me as if I had the plague."

To Rocco's horror, the boy with the bow took an arrow, fitted it in place, and drew the bow. He aimed it at Rocco's throat.

Rocco went white. "Don't play around with that," he croaked. "You could kill me."

"Do you have it?" asked Imma quietly.

"Have what?" he asked.

"Plague."

Rocco laughed nervously, and shook his head. The arrow moved down until it pointed at his feet. "No, I haven't got the plague," he said, wishing his voice were steadier. "I've never even seen it, where I come from. We've got plenty of other things, but not plague." The arrow moved up again. "But nothing serious," he added quickly. "Only measles and chicken pox, that sort of thing."

"They kill," murmured Imma.

"There was no disease in my city," said Rocco, carefully and clearly. "None at all."

Imma looked at the boy with the bow, and shook her head. He lowered it again, and Rocco relaxed.

"Come," said the girl. "We will take you to Petur."

"What'll he do?"

"Decide."

"Decide what?"

"If you be a spy."

"And what if he decides I am?"

"You'll be stoned."

She took his sleeve, briefly examined its

strange material, and pulled him towards the bridge. Rocco dragged back.

"What's stoned?" he asked. "I bet it's not what I think it is."

Imma smiled slightly and tossed her head backwards, indicating the bleached bones, white and broken between the boulders. "This is the stoning-ground," she said.

Rocco gave a howl of dismay, and pulled free. Immediately, several children jumped him from behind. He fell, dragging them down with him, and a girl laughed and kicked him hard in the abdomen. He curled up, retching. Everything became a blur, a savage turmoil of seething, grunting bodies, knees and stones in his back and shoulder blades, fingers tearing out his hair, knuckles in his throat, and pain. Then something crashed across his head, and he collapsed into utter dark.

Three

His first awareness was of a softness against his skin, and a feeling of being suffocated with smoke. His head throbbed, and he ached with bruising and cold. He raised his head, and the dark world spun. He waited until the dizziness passed, then sat up slowly, moaning with the effort and pain. Blurry-eyed, he stared into the surrounding dark.

A fire blazed in a low pit in the earth nearby, and two heavy blackened iron pots were suspended over it. He glanced up at the surrounding walls, shadowy and dim. The atmosphere was thick with choking smoke. He coughed and raised himself onto his knees, resting between moves. He realized he was naked, and the softness around him was furs. He crawled out from under them and staggered towards the fire. He craved a drink and fresh air. His throat burned, he felt stifled, and the fire wavered and danced in front of his eyes. He thought he was going to pass out again, and stepped backwards away from the flames. Then he saw her.

She was standing calmly on the other side of the fire, the light flickering gold across her rough woolen dress. She had black hair down to her waist, vivid blue eyes, and the kind of face Rocco dreamed about. He stared, entranced, and she smiled and held out some clothes. With horror, he remembered he was naked. His face flamed, and he made a frantic grab for one of the furs. He wrapped it about himself, then hesitated, summoning the courage to face her again. She was standing there still, her face grave, her eyes alight with humor, the clothes held out towards him.

"These be for you," she said. "A shirt and a coat of sheepskin, very fine and warm."

"Thanks," he said, avoiding meeting her eyes. He walked around the fire, the large fur clutched securely at his waist, and took the garments. They were heavy, coarse, and thick. The shirt was light grey, obviously well worn, but in good condition. The coat was luxurious, and dyed on the skin side with patterns of subtle green, ochre, and black.

"Where are my clothes?" he asked.

"Yours be taken to our priestess," she replied. She too spoke with a strange accent, like Tisha's. "They were wet," she added. "The children dragged you through the river."

"What's the priestess going to do with my clothes? Put a spell on them?"

She didn't answer, and Rocco turned away, retreated into the farthest shadows, and did his best to get dressed without dropping the fur. It was impossible, especially with clothes that were bulky, too big, and unfamiliar. He glanced back over his shoulder. She was sitting cross-legged on the floor, watching him.

"Look the other way," he said.

She smiled and turned her head. Quickly, he dropped the fur and scrambled into the shirt. It was a simple loose garment with no collar and long sleeves, and it reached almost to his knees. The neck opening had leather ties which he did his best to lace up in the darkness. He pulled the sleeveless sheepskin coat over the top, and went back to the fire.

The girl was stirring something in one of the iron pots, and there was a fragrance of fresh herbs she had just added. She glanced at Rocco, left the pot, went over to him, and without a word removed the coat.

He stared at her, wondering and speechless. She was even prettier close up. Her skin was flawless, rich in the fire's glow, and her mouth was curving and warm. She seemed about his age, and was slightly taller. As she leaned close to put the coat on him again, this time with the wool towards the inside, he blushed deeply and refused to meet her eyes. She stood close in front of him, undid the leather thongs on his shirt, and did them up again correctly. Her hands on his chest were light, quick, and businesslike, though she stayed unnecessarily close after she had finished, looking into his face with quiet laughter.

He turned aside, embarrassed, and saw a pair

of boots standing, warming by the fire. "Those be for you," she said.

He pulled them on, grateful for the warm, thick sheepskin inside. They were slightly too big for him, but very comfortable, and covered his legs to the knees. He bound them on with the leather cords she gave him, and stomped around the dirt floor. "They're good," he said. "Terrific. Thanks." He hesitated, looking at the girl. "Aren't there any trousers for me?"

"There be none to spare."

"I can't go without trousers."

She took a sharp knife from a sheath at her waist, and held it out towards him. Bewildered, he took it. Then she went to a shelf carved deep into the cave wall, took down a roll of buff-coloured hide, smooth and clean and softened with vegetable oils. She took as well a large curved bone needle, and a roll of fine leather cord. She handed it all to Rocco.

"Make yourself some then," she said. "It is Narvik's leather, but he won't mind."

Rocco stared at her across the roll of hide, and saw that she was serious. She sat by the fire again, her back to him, her shining blue-black hair streaming down almost to the floor. He placed the things back in the shelf and sat beside her. "I can't make clothes," he said.

She glanced sideways at him, amazed, not believing him. There was an uncomfortable silence.

"Who lives here?" he asked, after a while.

"I do," she replied. "And my father, Petur, and my brother Jakob. And Narvik, who will soon take a wife. And my little sister Toukie, who is sleeping in another cave tonight. Our mother died when she were born."

"What's your name?"

"Ilsabeth."

"Ilsabeth. I like that."

She looked at him sideways again, her full lips curved. Her eyes were like steady pieces of moonlight in the dark, luminous and cool. Her lashes were long and thick, and very black. Rocco swallowed nervously, and looked back at the fire. There was something cool and superior about her; a quiet confidence that he admired. He felt in awe of her.

"Don't you sleep?" he asked.

"Not tonight. Tonight I guard you."

He smiled slightly, though her face was grave. "Why?" he asked.

"Because we think you have come to spy on our valley, and take back knowledge of us to your tribe."

"I'm not a spy. My tribe wouldn't even believe in you."

"Your saying is hard."

"What do you mean?"

"Hard. I do not understand."

"I don't understand, either." He sighed and stood up. For the first time, he inspected his surroundings.

He had assumed he was in the same cave he had often dreamed about. To his surprise, it was a different one. This cave was larger, though the pottery and weapons it contained were similar. There was no furniture, and the only storage places were deep alcoves and shelves carved into the cave walls. On the shelves were metal pots, primitive clay lamps, pottery bowls, and bone spoons. There were other things too, but Rocco couldn't identify them in the changing, hazy dark.

There was the one pile of straw in the back of the cave, with several large furs thrown over it. Rocco wondered whether the whole family slept together. Dried grass and herbs were strewn across the floor, and a pleasant aroma wafted up as Rocco walked on them. But nothing could disguise the acrid, suffocating smoke. It spread a gloomy film right across the cave, making everything indistinct, before it billowed out through the gap above the skins covering the entrance. The only brightness was the fire, and the occasional flicker of light on a knife or smooth-glazed jar.

Weapons hung on pegs driven into the sooty walls, and the firelight gleamed on smoothly curving bows, sleek spears, and on the metal tips of arrows. Vegetables hung in bunches from leather strips suspended across the roof, and Rocco made out carrots, turnips, and onions.

He went over to the cave entrance, pushed aside the heavy skins, and looked out. The sudden spaciousness shocked him. He was standing on a ledge near the top of the cliff. At his feet, and all around, stretched the vast velvet night; the river far below, gurgling and rushing across the black plain; the mountains, clear and majestic under the starry sky; and there was the wind, the eternal wind, howling like a lonely living thing through the valley. It whistled across the cliff face, lifted Rocco's damp hair, and made the wind chimes hum.

Rocco gazed up at the brilliant stars, the wide awesome silences, and wondered whether he was in a real place, or whether this was just an incredibly vivid dream. It didn't feel like a dream. It didn't have that shadowy, insubstantial quality of a dream, or that underlying sense of unreality. The mountains, the smoky tang in the cold wind, the ringing of wind chimes, the softness of his fur boots, and the smell of the leather hides behind his back, were all concrete, clear, and totally real.

He felt a soft movement behind him, and was aware of Ilsabeth standing close. He noticed she held a long hunting bow, with an arrow in place.

"Can you use that?" he asked.

"I be one of the best shooters in the tribe," she replied, cooly, her eyes on his face. He didn't doubt her.

"Don't worry," he said, smiling. "I don't plan on running anywhere."

They went back inside the cave, and she hung the bow across two pegs. They sat near the fire together, their hands outstretched towards the flames.

"What is your name?" she asked.

"Rocco."

"Do your people be traveling gypsies?"

"No. We live in a city."

"Then how is it you don't make your own clothes? Is your city a trading center?"

"Yes. We trade there."

"And you came here to see what we have to trade?"

He sighed, and ran his hands through his hair. "Ilsabeth, I don't know why I came here," he said. "I can't explain."

"Is there sickness in your town? Do you be looking for somewhere safe to live?"

"No. I'm not looking for anything. I can't explain. If I could, I would. But I can't."

"Were you eating those herbs and roots that make people forget?"

"No. Please don't ask questions, Ilsabeth. I can't answer them."

"Who be the people who traded you your clothes? They be different from anything traded here."

"Levi. A tribe called Levi traded me my clothes."

"They never come here."

"I guess they ran out of gas."

"Your saying is hard."

Rocco buried his head in his hands, and groaned. His head ached, and his ribs were sore. He pressed his fingers into his eyes, willing himself back to his own room at home. But when he looked up he saw only the smoky cave and Ilsabeth's face, flushed and golden in the fire's glow.

"I be sorry," she said softly, smiling. "I be not asking any more questions."

"Thanks. And thanks for these clothes. They're fine. I like them better than mine."

"They were Torun's," she said, the smile fading from her face. "All his things were fine. He used to go far, even beyond The Voidances, and trade grain for woven clothes and sheepskin. It is good for you that his clothes be yours now."

"What happened to him?"

"He fell from a high mountain place, and his neck broke. He lived seven days, then — then he died. That were last autumn, twelve full moons ago."

"He was your brother?" asked Rocco gently.

She shook her head. "He did be promised with me," she said. "He were going to be my husband, in the spring."

It was Rocco's turn to look amazed. "You were going to be married?"

"That is the custom in our tribe, when a woman and a man want each other."

"It's my tribe's custom, too, but we don't marry so. . . . How old are you, Ilsabeth?"

"I were fifteen, two full moons ago." She gave him a small smile. "You do be very like Torun," she murmured. "When Imma and the children brought you here, bleeding and hurt, I did think you were him again, and I did nearly die for fear and joy."

"Sorry I disappointed you," he said, returning her smile.

"I be not disappointed."

He tore his gaze from hers and looked into the flames.

There was stamping behind them, and the skins in the entrance were swept suddenly aside. Rocco jumped up as a bitter wind rushed across the cave. The fire leapt madly, smoke swirled, and then the skins swung closed again.

A man stood beside them. He was not tall or imposing, but there was something arresting about his fierce, calm face, his penetrating gaze, and his strong, unsmiling mouth. He was not yet forty, but his shoulder-length hair was iron-grey, and his hands, when he held them out to the fire, were scarred and roughened by work. He had a dark, swarthy beard, and his eyes were steely blue. He wore a thick fur coat, leather trousers, and high fur-lined boots.

Ilsabeth took a pottery bowl, dipped it in one of the pots, wiped it, and handed it to the man. He curved his hands around it to warm them, and crouched by the fire. His eyes never left Rocco's face.

"Sit again," he said, and his voice was surprisingly soft and low.

Rocco sat with his arms around his knees. His legs had pins and needles in them, and his head still throbbed. He eyed the man's hot drink, and glanced pleadingly at Ilsabeth. She sat opposite him, watching him through the fire. He felt isolated and alone.

"My name is Petur," said the man, sipping the hot liquid in his bowl. "I will hear your words. I must know who you be, where you be from, and why you have come. It is for me to decide whether you be for us, or against us. Choose your words carefully, with wisdom and truth. No one else will speak for you."

Rocco swallowed, and met the man's eyes. "I'll do my best," he promised. "But I don't think you're going to understand."

"I understand truth," said Petur quietly. "Begin. Tell me your name."

"Rocco."

"Your place."

"Tolver. A city called Tolver."

"How many days' journey?"

"What do you mean?"

"How many days have you walked? How far is it between Tolver and here?"

"A long way . . . I didn't count the days."

"But there were many."

"Oh, yes. Hundreds."

"Then tell me this, Rocco: If you came so far, walked so many days, how is it you have no cart, no supplies of water or food, no furs for warmth, no hides for shelter, no weapons? I have seen your garments, your feet. They were clean. Not a day's journey have you done, Rocco. I ask you one more time: Where is your place?"

"I can't tell you."

Petur looked at him closely. His blue eyes bored into Rocco's head, probing, testing, weighing. "Your face is not that of a madman," he said, after a while.

Rocco grinned. "That's encouraging."

"I do not make a joke, Rocco. Madmen I have seen. They too have strange stories to tell, truths that be not truths, that only their eyes see. Or they say nothing. What do you be, Rocco? You come to us from nowhere, with nothing but your strange, beautiful garments and your clean bare feet, and you tell us you have walked a hundred days.

"Do you know what is beyond this place, Rocco? Beyond this circle of mountains? Stones and dust. Dust and stones. You walk in them for a hundred days and more, and still it is stones and dust. And you came across that without food, without protection, without weapons, nor anything to trade, and you will not tell me how.

"I tell you how you came here. From a far place beyond The Voidances, from a city destroyed by hunger or war or disease, you were brought to this place in a cart by your tribe, and left here to spy out our valley while your tribe waits, hiding. And you will see our place, and judge our strength, and count our pots of grain and our animals, and you will go back to your people. You will tell them we be not too strong for them, and they will easily overcome us, and our homes and crops and goats will support them. And they will come and destroy us, and live in our place. I know this. It has happened before, in the Bad Time. But it will not happen again."

"I'm not a spy," said Rocco calmly, though his heart thundered in his ribs, and sweat broke out on his palms. "I'm not a spy. If I was, I wouldn't walk down here in broad daylight, in full view of everyone."

"You would," said Petur thoughtfully, "if you were a clever spy. You would come openly, and pretend to be a trader, perhaps."

"I've brought nothing to trade."

"Perhaps you bring skills, then, that we do not have. Perhaps you be a weaver, or a worker in wood."

"No."

"Then why have you come?"

"I don't know."

Petur stood up and placed his cup on an

earthen shelf. He lifted one of the long hunting knives from its place on the cave wall, and weighed it carefully in his hands, his eyes on Rocco's face.

"You fight, Rocco?" he asked. "Be you skilled with knives? Skilled at killing quick and quiet?"

Rocco stood up and began pacing the floor, his fists clenched under his arms. His head was pounding. Fear began to crawl through him, gathering like a spring in the pit of his stomach. A part of him seemed to float apart, aloof and amused, and mocked him for not rushing out over the edge of the cliff, and ending the dream. But all the rest of him believed that what was happening was real, and he was desperately afraid. He stopped pacing, and stood in front of Petur.

"I'm not a spy," he said again. "I could tell you where I come from, but it would be worse than lies to you. I can't tell you why I'm here because I don't know. I don't understand how I got here. I didn't come with any intentions of hurting anyone, or stealing anything, or telling anyone about you. If it's any comfort to you, no one would believe me, anyway. I didn't want to come here, and I don't want to stay. I don't care about you or your people, or your grain and goats. I just want to go. I'm not a spy, Petur. I just want this thing to finish, to be over and done with. I don't know where I am, and it scares me."

"You do be in the cliff dwellings of Anshur," said Petur gently, putting the knife back in its place. "I tell you a truth, Rocco: I do not know what to make of you."

"Just let me go, then," said Rocco desperately, "and stop questioning me."

"And what will you do if I let you go?"

"Do? I'll walk! Just walk. You'll never see me again."

Petur watched Rocco's white face, and compassion softened his hard features. "I think you should sleep now," he said softly. "It will be dawn soon. You too, Ilsabeth."

Ilsabeth went over to the pile of furs, brushed the dust off her bare feet, and slipped in. Rocco blinked at Petur. "Where's my bed?" he asked. "I'm not sleeping with her, am I?"

"You can sleep on the floor if you want to," said Petur, sitting down and making himself comfortable by the fire, "but the bed will be warmer."

"I can't argue with that," murmured Rocco, crossing the cave and easing himself down into the warmth beside Ilsabeth. She turned her back on him, dragging all the furs with her. He pulled the top one back, spread it over himself, and lay tensely looking up at the smoky ceiling. Something in him wanted to laugh. He glanced at Petur, sitting guard by the fire, sipping at another drink from the iron pot. Then he turned his head and looked at Ilsabeth's long black hair mingling with the shining of the furs. She rubbed his leg with her foot, and he realized he still had on his boots. He did laugh then, quietly to himself.

I don't believe this, he thought. But I wouldn't mind if it was real. I wouldn't mind at all.

Four

For a long time Rocco lay awake, listening to the wild, hollow sound of the wind wailing in the valley below, and the golden crackling of the cave fire. His head still ached, and he hurt all over from the beating the children had given him. He slid further under the furs, careful not to disturb Ilsabeth, who already slept.

Petur began working on a small dried animal pelt, scraping the skin even and smooth with his knife, then softening it by rubbing it with a small stone. The sound of his work was soothing and quiet, and Rocco relaxed as he listened. After a while he dozed, and the sound of the wind and Petur's work mingled with the sounds of his dreams. Through it all there came sometimes the deep ringing of the wind chimes, silvery and clear. There were voices, softly spoken but urgent, and the tones drifted through his dreams, pricking his fear. He woke, suddenly, his throat dry and raw, his head throbbing. The murmuring voices went on, and he realized there were two other people in the cave.

He turned his head, quietly, and saw two youths talking with Petur. One was sitting opposite him across the fire, his back to Rocco; the other, a boy Rocco's age, stood leaning against the cave wall. He had strange amber-colored eyes, and long straight black hair past his shoulders.

". . . and the armband. What did she say of that?" It was Petur's voice.

"Nothing, Father," replied the youth sitting near the fire. "She looked at it for a long time, and said not to question him."

"It is too late. I have."

"We came back as fast as we could. There were no moon, and we lost the path."

"I know. It is not an easy walk, from her cave. But the armband is of a strange and excellent metalcraft. She must have said something about it."

"Nothing." That came from the youth leaning against the wall. "She said to keep him here until she comes. She said we are to ask him nothing. She said his sayings would be too hard for us."

Rocco closed his eyes again, and wished desperately that his headache would go. The voices droned on, and he dozed. Words came to him, fluttered dimly on the edges of his pain, and vanished. Then he heard a name.

"Ayoshe."

He sat up suddenly, and the cave swam. Petur looked across. "Be you ill, Rocco?"

Rocco dragged himself out of the bed, stumbled across to the fire, and sat down with his head in his hands. "Who's Ayoshe?" he asked hoarsely.

"You know of her?" Petur's voice was harsh, demanding.

"I don't know. I've got an awful headache. Have you got any aspirin?"

"We have rosemary tea for that," Petur replied. "Ilsabeth will prepare you some in the morning."

Rocco looked at the youth sitting beside him. He was in his late teens, a good-looking younger version of Petur, with a short dark beard and black, knife-cut hair. "I greet you, Rocco," he said, smiling. "My name is Narvik."

"Hi." Rocco tried to smile, but his whole face ached, and he winced instead. He glanced at the boy standing up. The boy frowned suddenly, and his face went red with anger. He turned on Petur, furious.

"He's wearing Torun's clothes! They were mine! Set aside for me!"

"Peace, Jakob," murmured Petur, throwing a piece of strange round fuel on the fire. "You can have them, after him."

"But they were mine!"

"I said, peace!"

Jakob flung himself down by the fire opposite Rocco, and glared at him with murder in his eyes.

"You know Ayoshe?" Petur asked Rocco again, quietly.

"No. But I feel as if I should. It's not the name,

it's the feeling of the name. Strength. Safety. I can't explain it. It's a feeling, that's all."

Astounded, Petur looked a long time into Rocco's face. At last he said slowly, "Ayoshe lives in a cave half a morning's walk up the mountains. She is our guardian, teacher, healer, priestess, and friend. She is all joy, all wisdom, all strength. She is Ayoshe."

"Are you in love with her?" asked Rocco.

Petur laughed, a great roar of laughter that startled his sons and woke Ilsabeth. Still chuckling, and without answering, he got up and went outside, and they heard the wind chimes clang as he brushed past them.

Rocco looked at Narvik. "What did I say that was so funny?" he asked.

Narvik chuckled. "You'll find out in the morning," he said, "when you meet Ayoshe."

"You do be a cockroach, Rocco!" yelled Jakob furiously. "Can't you walk like a human being?"

Rocco gripped the flimsy leather strip that was all he had between himself and the terrifying drop, and shuffled along the wooden plank that bridged two ledges on the cliff. "Give me a few days and I will," he said over his shoulder. He stepped thankfully onto the wide path on the other side. Jakob strode along the plank, pushed past Rocco, almost knocking him over the edge, and went on ahead. Rocco clenched his fists and followed him.

The rest of the path sloped sharply down, and was cut at times into rough irregular steps. Sometimes it widened into ledges, and Rocco glanced briefly into other caves as he passed. Sometimes the skins were lifted aside, and children, terribly familiar, grinned out at him. Sometimes he brushed past wind chimes, setting them ringing out across the peaceful valley. It was early morning, and the cliff face was in shadow still; but the valley on the other side of the river, and the mountains opposite, were tawny in the early morning sun. It was a wild, tranquil place, brown and bleak and beautiful. Rocco wished it were Ilsabeth with him, and not Jakob.

Safely on the ground at last, Rocco looked back up the way he had come, all along the earthen steps and primitive bridges, past the yawning caves with their smoky fires. There were twelve caves altogether, some small and obviously used as storehouses; but there were six large caves where families lived.

"You'll see everyone else at the Talking-Stone," said Jakob, as he and Rocco walked towards the riverbend, "when they decide about you."

"What do you mean — decide about me?" asked Rocco, running to keep up with him, hampered by the big boots. "I thought your father decided about me last night. You're not doing anything."

"We be deciding, all of us, what will happen with you," said Jakob coldly. "And I know where I will cast my stone."

"What do you mean?"

"Casting stones. Deciding. We all do, everyone past their thirteenth summer. We each have a stone, and if we place it inside the circle, you be free to live among us. And if we place it outside the circle, you be not. The biggest pile of stones is the deciding-pile."

"I see," said Rocco. "And what happens if they're all outside the circle? I'm free to go?"

Jakob gave a harsh laugh and strode on rapidly, past the walled garden. But for a fraction of a second, his gaze had slid towards the stoning-ground.

"That's not fair!" yelled Rocco, stumbling after him. "You don't even know me! None of you do!"

"Nothing is fair!" spat Jakob. "You be not fair, coming into our valley with no reason, no explanation, nothing. You could carry plague. You could wipe out our whole tribe. And you say we be not fair! Well, nothing's fair. Nothing is a gift, nothing is won easily. You want your freedom, your life, you'll have to fight for it. You'll have your turn on the Talking-Stone. Then we decide."

"You've already decided."

"So I have."

"Why? Because I've got the clothes you wanted? If that's why you hate me you can have them back. I don't want them, anyway. I never wanted clothes from a corpse."

Jakob stopped walking, and waited for Rocco to draw alongside. Then he hit Rocco across the face, hard. For an instant Rocco was going to hit him back; but something in Jakob's face stopped him.

"Never talk again like that, of Torun," said

Jakob quietly. "He is no corpse. He is my friend, free now. In the wind. It is an honor for you to wear his clothes."

He walked on, and Rocco watched him disappear beyond the riverbend, where the barren soil and fierce bronze grass gave way to mountain stones. Then Rocco went and sat alone on the rocks by the river, staring at the water and the distant hills, seeing nothing.

He did not know how long he sat there. An hour, perhaps, in his own world. Here, there were no hours. Here there were full moons, summers, and distances of days. Here there were Talking-Stones, and fatal circles in the dust. And his mind whirled in circles, terrible circles that were boundless and spanned centuries. He covered his face with his hands, anguished.

A small thin arm slipped around his neck, and a little body wriggled next to his on the rock. He smelled herbs and smoke, and felt long tousled hair brush the back of his wrist. He took down his hands, and smiled.

"Hello, Tisha."

She grinned like an imp. "I saw them drown you in the river," she said.

"They were just dragging me across, they didn't drown me," he replied. "It'll take more than a bunch of kids to finish me off." His face was suddenly hard, his green eyes bitter in the cold bright light. Tisha said nothing, but her arm tightened about his neck.

"Tell me about the Talking-Stone, Tisha," he said.

"It's a place where people stand and talk," she

said. "And you can say anything you like, for as long as you like, and no one is allowed to stop you or argue with you until you be finished."

"What happens if someone stands on the Talking-Stone and says nothing at all?" asked Rocco.

Tisha giggled. "Then it wouldn't be a Talking-Stone, would it?" she said. She got up, jumped onto a flat rock in front of him and did a mad little dance, waving her arms and spinning like a wild golden sprite in the morning.

"I've got a dancing-stone," she sang, leaping from rock to rock with the agility of a goat. Rocco watched, amused and smiling. There was something intensely alive about Tisha, something animal and free and unspoiled that delighted him.

From the cliffs behind them one of the wind chimes tolled out, rhythmically and slow. Startled, Tisha stopped and looked at Rocco. "That be the signal to meet at the Talking-Stone," she said. "It's your turn to talk, I think."

Tensely, Rocco stood up and began to walk back to the cliff. Tisha skipped beside him, swinging on his hand. "Will you talk," she asked, doing another dance, "or will you be funny, and not say anything?"

"I think I'll be funny," he said, "but I've a feeling no one will laugh."

"I will," she said.

The entire population of the valley was there. There were three women and two men around Petur's age, and one very old woman. Of the twenty others, Narvik was the oldest, and he was nineteen. All the rest were young people and children. Rocco guessed the entire tribe consisted of only a few families, and most of the parents had died. It was a small tribe, isolated, solitary, and private. He felt like an intruder.

The tribe was sitting in a semicircle on the dusty ground in front of a large flat rock. Only Petur was standing. Everyone was silent. Even the smallest children were quiet, watching Rocco out of solemn, curious eyes. Petur beckoned Rocco to him.

"We be all here, now," he said, and Rocco scanned the group wondering which of the women was Ayoshe. He wondered if she was the stunning woman with long red hair and penetrating grey eyes. The woman looked at him and smiled.

"These be my people," went on Petur, in solemn tones. "This is my family, my life. This valley called Anshur, these caves and crops and goats, be all we have. We guard them with our lives. We do not know whether you come as a friend, or enemy. If friend, you will be permitted to stay a short time as our guest, or you will be free to leave. If enemy, we cannot let you live. According to your own words, we will decide. Now is your time to talk."

Petur sat down then, and nodded for Rocco to step up onto the stone. Rocco stood where he was, deathly white, his throat pounding. He couldn't have spoken, even if he had wanted to.

The people waited, sitting in silence until the silence grew too long, and Tisha began to giggle.

Imma stood up and took her away. No one else moved.

"It would not be right for me to stand on the Talking-Stone," said Rocco at last, in a low voice. "I can tell you nothing."

"Is that your only word?" asked Petur.

Rocco nodded.

"This is a serious time for you, Rocco," said Petur heavily, standing up.

"I know that," said Rocco. He thought, grimly, I could wake up dead.

"And you still say nothing?"

"There is nothing I can say that you will understand."

"Then we will decide," said Petur, and drew a circle in the dust at Rocco's feet.

One by one the older children and the adults came forward. Ilsabeth placed her stone inside the circle; so did Narvik. They were the only ones. Then Petur cast his stone, dropping it deliberately just outside the circle's edge. Ten stones were outside, and only the old woman was left with her stone still in her hand.

She stood up slowly, with an easy grace, and came forwards to the circle. She never looked at Rocco. She crouched there in front of him, her stone poised in her palm above the yellow earth. Then, with her other hand, she gathered up all the stones, placed them carefully in the center of the circle, her own on top, and wiped the circle smooth. It was like a ritual, deliberate and meaningful. She spread her hands over the pile of stones, said a few words in a language Rocco didn't know, and stood up. She turned and faced the silent witnesses.

"There will be no judgment on Rocco," she said. Her words were quiet, effective, and final. "There will be no questions, no answers, no arguments. He is free to stay a time as our guest. Consider him my son."

To Rocco's amazement, without a single protest the people all stood up and left. Only Petur came over to the old woman, placed his big hands on her thin shoulders, and kissed her cheek. Then he too went away. The men and women went to the caves, or to work in the garden. The children ran off, laughing, and some of the young people climbed up to the caves to get weapons to go hunting. Jakob got his bow and arrows and strode off alone towards the mountains.

For a long time Rocco stood behind the old woman, watching the sun cast lights and shades across her long white hair. Her back was straight, her head held high, and she gave the impression of being quite tall. But she was slightly shorter than Rocco. She wore a rough robe tied at her narrow waist with a leather strip. Rocco saw a small soft leather bag, dyed red, hanging from her belt, and a knife with a handle of bone. Her feet were bare, the soles thick like old leather. The hands at her sides were long, delicate, and finely wrinkled. Her skin was brown, weathered many years in wind and sun. Even before he saw her face, Rocco was in awe of her. He grew uncomfortable, wondering why she waited. Perhaps there was a custom here he didn't understand. She had probably saved his life; there must be something he should say.

She turned then, and for the first time looked

into his face. For an instant her eyes widened, and shock swept through her. The next moment she was calm, controlled, slightly smiling.

Rocco met her striking dark eyes, and the power of her swept over him like a flood. He felt naked, peeled open layer after layer, until his innermost being, his deepest fears and doubts, were all laid bare, and known. It was not an enjoyable feeling, but neither was it painful. When the shock of it was past, he felt cleansed, all the apprehension and fear gone out of him. It was as if he was at last fully known, and fully understood.

He smiled then, and held out his hand towards her. "Hello, Ayoshe," he said.

She took his hand in both hers, and her smile broke across all her face.

"Hello, Rocco," she said. "I welcome you to Anshur. I'm sorry I wasn't here earlier. I might have prevented some of your distress."

"I survived," he said lightly.

Her eyes bored into him. "Yes. I think you always will."

She turned then, and began walking back up the valley, past the cave dwellings and the enclosed garden, and on beyond the riverbend. Rocco hurried after her. They walked in silence for a while, and she led him up into the foothills of the mountains, along a steep dusty path between the rocks.

"What am I supposed to do, now I'm here?" Rocco asked, trying not to sound out of breath.

"What are your skills?" she asked.

He looked sideways into her incredible old

face, and said: "Do you want the truth, or do you want what I think I should say?"

She stopped walking then, and faced him squarely. "Always truth between us," she said.

"Good. Can we sit down and talk? I'm not as fit as you."

Ayoshe accepted that without a hint of a smile, and they sat beside each other on a jutting rock, facing down to the river.

"I'm not really skilled at basic survival stuff," said Rocco. "I ride a bike, work in a takeaway place weekends, I'm a terrific swimmer, and I'm not bad at fixing minor electrical problems. You know, broken plugs, light switches, and things."

She nodded gravely, her eyes veiled under the heavy lids, her strong, determined mouth slightly smiling. He realized with a shock that her face was hardly wrinkled. Her fine brown skin shone across her high cheekbones, and her brow was smooth and high. Her nose was large and slightly hooked, her whole face strong and dignified. It was easy to understand her influence in the valley, easy to feel her strength. Yet there was a warmth in her, a humor and a joy that drew Rocco like a magnet. He knew that with her he could say anything, do anything, be truly himself; and he would always be accepted.

She glanced at him, her eyes dancing. "Don't test me too far, Rocco," she said. "Your truth is hard for me. I'm not sure your skills will be much use to us. Our electrical problems are very few. What are you like with weapons?"

"I've won tournaments with my bow," he smiled.

Ayoshe shot him a swift, shrewd look. "Keep that under the furs," she advised. "Surprises are very effective here."

"Why are you helping me, Ayoshe?" he asked. "I've got a feeling you know something I don't."

"And you know something I don't," she said, "so we're equal, don't you think?"

"Equal, like an eagle and an ant," said Rocco. He added hurriedly, "I'm the ant."

"Some ants fly, too," she said. "And now you must go back to Petur. He has need of you."

"How do you know? Got a two-way radio?"

"I know these things, Rocco." Her smile was brilliant.

"Don't tell me," he said. "Extrasensory perception. You're like my grandmother."

"Goodbye, Rocco."

It was a dismissal. He stood up and began walking back. After a while he turned and waved to her. She lifted her hand, but the gesture was a blessing and not a farewell. He walked on, still smiling, amazed, overcome by the feeling that she had known him all his life.

Five

"What is your decision, Rocco?" asked Petur, handing him a pottery bowl of hot food. "Will you stay with us a while, or go?"

"Stay, I guess," said Rocco, sniffing the bowl suspiciously. "It's a long walk to anywhere else, and your bus service is terrible." He picked a small portion of fried batter out of the bowl and bit into it. It was hard and crunchy, and very salty. He smiled at Ilsabeth across the fire. "Not bad," he said. "A bit salty, though. What is it?"

"Fried crickets," she said, and Rocco was nearly sick. He put his bowl on the cave floor between himself and Jakob, and stood up. "I think I'll just have a drink," he said. Four-year-old Toukie ran to get a clean bowl for him.

"It's their blood that's salty," explained Petur. "You'll get used to it. It is good for you."

Rocco rescued the bowl from Toukie, who was about to drop it in the pot, scooped himself out a drink, and went to the cave entrance. He pushed aside the heavy skins and went out. He rinsed his mouth with some of the herb tea, and spat it out over the edge. Then he sat down to drink, leaning against the sun-warmed wall, grateful for the fresh breeze.

The autumn skies were clear, the sun directly overhead, yet the air was cold. He was glad that the red-headed woman, Eden, had brought him a spare pair of soft leather trousers from her cave. She had a son, Jaim, slightly older than Rocco, who had given several of his garments for the tribe's guest. Rocco was grateful, knowing now that clothes were laboriously handmade, and precious. Everything woven had been traded for.

He sipped the pungent, pepperminty tea, and looked across the valley. Across the river a small boy was herding goats, and their bleating carried over on the wind, and sounded peaceful and homely. Rocco had the feeling that he had been here before, that it was all familiar and known to him. Even his clothes felt comfortable, the furs and leathers smelling pleasant and good. He wondered if it was only in his dreams that he had come, and if so what kind of dreams they were. He closed his hands around the pottery bowl, warming them, and watched the shepherd boy and the goats, and listened to the wind humming in the wind chimes. The sun slowly warmed his face, and he leaned back against the cliff wall, relaxed and at peace. He had no doubt now that all this was real; he wondered only what kind of reality it was, what dimension and time. Somehow, he didn't care. He was here and, apart from Jakob and the crickets, everything entranced him.

Ilsabeth came out and sat cross-legged beside him, her knee touching his. "Father wants to talk with you, when you be ready," she said. "He said there be many things for you to learn."

Rocco grinned. "That's for sure."

"He doesn't mean the big things, like hunting, tanning hides, and making weapons," she said. "It's the small things. Things even the little children have to learn."

"I realize that," said Rocco. "The basic things, like eating crickets, and how to use your toilet pit without falling in."

"Did you?" she cried, appalled.

He laughed. "Almost."

"Talk with Father," she smiled. "He'll tell you about these things."

Rocco drained his bowl, and they went back into the dim cave. Narvik was gathering up the bowls ready for washing in the river. "Be you sure you don't want to eat?" he asked Rocco, looking worried.

"I'm not hungry," Rocco lied. "I'll wait for dinner."

"You'll love the feast tonight," said Narvik, as he left the cave. He grinned back over his shoulder. "It's rats."

Ilsabeth looked at Rocco's face, and laughed. "No it isn't," she said. "It's rabbits. Imma and the children trapped them this morning."

Rocco heaved a sigh of relief, and dropped to the smooth floor near the fire. Petur sat beside him and handed him a knife. The blade was about twenty centimeters long, and the handle was of animal horn. The handle was made smooth on one side, and etched with pictures of deer, lizards, and fierce birds.

"That is yours," said Petur. "Narvik will show you how to make a leather sheath for it. Always wear it on you, especially when you leave the caves. In the mountains there be wildcat, wolves, scorpions, and bears.

"For the rest of today, and all the next five days, you stay with Imma and the children. They will teach you everything you need to know about our ways. There is only one place you will not go: The cave where the grain is stored. Our grain is our life. If it is ruined, in winter we starve.

"You do not enter other caves unless you be invited. You do not even look in them as you go past. Our caves be our homes. They be private.

"And now I must ask you a thing, Rocco, even though our Mother has forbidden it. It is the only question I shall ask. I need to know how much you know, and what skills you have. How different is our valley from your place, and what did you do there?"

"It's very different," said Rocco carefully. "We don't hunt for food, or grow our own grain. We don't use weapons, we don't prepare skins or make our own clothes. I went to school there. That is a place where I learned to read and write, and to gain skills for later on. I can't tell you more than that. I'm sorry."

For a long time Petur was silent. He sat staring into the fire, his hands folded quietly in front of him. His face betrayed no emotion, but a small nerve twitched on his jaw.

"Thank you for your words," he said at last. "I honor them. It may be that you do have something you can teach to us. I myself write, but only very little. Perhaps it is time we all learned."

"Anything I can do here, I will," said Rocco. "I don't want to be a burden to you, to any of you. I want to do my share."

Petur nodded slowly. "Those be good words to hear," he murmured. "But first, there be skills you have to learn. When your five days with Imma and the children be over, you will have five days with Jakob. You will learn to make pottery, to cure and tan skins, and divide meat for food. You will learn the ways we cook, care for weapons, and how to use a bow and arrow. Finally, you will go on a hunt with Jakob, for wildcat. It will be dangerous, but it will be your most valuable learning time."

Rocco glanced across the cave at Jakob, sitting in the smoky shadows sharpening arrowheads on a flat stone. Jakob looked up from his work, his face glistening with sweat, and his fierce eyes burned into Rocco. He half smiled and held an arrow to the firelight, tested its point with his finger, then stood up, satisfied. He put the stone back on a shelf, slid the arrows into a quiver on his back, and picked up his bow. Without a word he walked in front of Rocco, so close that Rocco was forced back to give him room, and went out of the cave. He left behind a grim, uncomfortable silence.

Rocco looked at his hands, clenched and white

in front of him, and didn't dare look at Petur. "I'd rather not go hunting," he said in a low voice. "Not with him, anyway."

Petur stood up and threw some more fuel on the fire. The light leapt and flashed around the walls, and sparks flew.

"If I say you hunt with Jakob, you hunt with Jakob," he said.

"Ayoshe said I was to be treated as her son," returned Rocco. "I'll ask her."

"In this valley, Ayoshe's word is always the last," Petur said quietly, though his face was dark with anger. "But while she is in her cave and you be in mine, you do as I say."

Rocco stood up, collected a fur jerkin from an alcove in the wall, and put it on. He was about to leave, his hand already on the skins across the entrance, when Petur called him back.

"You do be our guest, Rocco," he said, no longer angry. "I cannot force you to do anything. But if you be as untrained in our ways as you say you be, I urge you to take all my advice. Otherwise, I think you will not survive."

Rocco stood still for a few moments, then pushed aside the heavy skins, and went out.

The next five days were the hardest of Rocco's life. Never had he been so desperate, so challenged, so determined to win. The children were merciless. They guided him up the most treacherous places in the mountains they knew, and left him there to find his own way back. They sent him into dangerous parts of the river to check nonexistent fishing traps. They tricked him into running down naked into the swimming hole when it was the women's time to bathe. They teased him with cockroaches and snakes, and ate live crickets in front of him. They tested him to his limits, humiliated, tormented, and adored him. And when he still came back for more, they taught him how to trap rabbits, to grind corn, to milk goats and make butter and cheese, and to collect animal dung for fuel. He learned how to trap and gut fish, clean insects off the garden vegetables, and kill scorpions. The children showed him where the wild herbs grew, and where to gather moss and dry grass for the beds. They showed him the high places where the buzzards built their nests, and taught him to recognise the tracks of goats, wildcats, and wolves.

And they showed him Ayoshe's cave.

In the afternoon of the fifth day they went there. It was a warm day with no wind, and for the first time in the valley Rocco went barefoot, and wore only his soft leather trousers and woven shirt. Imma took her bow, and the oldest boy, Wyll, carried a short spear. All the older children carried knives in leather sheaths tied to their belts, and one of the boys carried a club.

It was a steep, difficult path up the mountain. Ten-year-old Wyll led the way, keeping a lookout for slips on the path, and wild animals. Rocco walked at the back of the group, with Imma. He had come to admire Imma. She was strong for her age, and expert at killing and skinning rabbits quickly and efficiently. She was tireless, fearless, and inspiring. It was she, more than any of them, who goaded Rocco into pushing himself to his limits. There was nothing Imma wouldn't attempt, no challenge she wouldn't meet head-on, and she expected the same nerve from Rocco. And Rocco had given it. He admired Imma's gentle side, too; her concern for all the children, and her astounding knowledge of wildlife and plants. It was hard for Rocco to realize that she was only twelve years old.

All the children seemed older than they were; all were daring and strong, and wise beyond their years. Even the eight little ones, right down to three-year-old Morg, were plucky and resourceful. They were all incredibly fit, and ran leaping and yelling up the mountain like a herd of noisy goats. Only Morg lagged behind, slipping and slithering on the dusty slopes, and screeching at the others to wait. Rocco picked him up and swung him high up onto his shoulders, and Morg screamed with delight, and grabbed fistfuls of Rocco's black curly hair.

"Don't piddle down my back," warned Rocco, stumbling on a stone and almost overbalancing. "And stop jiggling or we'll fall."

He stopped, noticing a tough, leafy plant with a white flower growing between some rocks to the left of the path. He pointed it out to Imma, who was walking behind him. "Isn't that angelica?" he asked. "You said you wanted some more, to dry."

She looked to where he pointed, and nodded, pleased. She left the path, clambered over the rocks to the plant, and cut off the top tender twigs with her knife. She tucked them into her belt, and came back. She was chewing one of the leaves, and she offered one to Rocco. He took it, sniffed its strong, pleasant aroma, and put it in his mouth. It tasted of licorice.

"Do you remember what it's for?" she asked, smiling up at him through her tangled hair. "In medicine?"

He thought for a few moments, while they labored up a steep, corkscrew track leading to a ridge. "Toothache," he said, between breaths. "And against poisons. And plague."

Imma shot him a surprised look of approval. "Don't tell Ayoshe how much you've learned," she said. "She'll be wanting to train you, instead of Ilsabeth."

"No she won't," said Rocco, stopping a moment on the slippery slope to rest. "I'm not going to be a healer. I'm going to be a hunter."

"You be needing to kill rabbits quicker then," she said with a small smile.

The path was almost vertical now, and they needed hands as well as feet to climb. Imma glanced back every now and again to see how Rocco was managing. To her surprise, he was right behind her, with Morg clinging to his back. Five days ago Rocco would have collapsed in a heap halfway back. Now only the sweat on his face gave any hint of his fatigue.

A cool wind rushed across their heads, and they came out onto the top of the ridge. Rocco stopped and straightened up, breathing deeply, and looked out across the view. For the first time, he saw beyond the mountains. And what he saw astounded him.

For as far as his eyes could see, from the foothills of the mountains to the distant haze of the horizon, stretched a vast desert. He had never seen such emptiness, such utter desolation. There was nothing there but dust, flat unending dust, with scudding dust clouds driven by the wind, and strange distant canyons. It was a wilderness, bleak and lonely and terrifying.

Rocco shivered and turned to Imma. "Is that all there is, beyond this place?" he asked.

She nodded. "They be The Voidances," she said, and started walking out along the windy ridge.

He followed, suddenly bitterly cold, keeping his eyes on the narrow track ahead. Morg began to wriggle on his back. "The cave!" he yelled, pulling at Rocco's neck, and almost choking him. "Around there!"

Rocco put him down, and the little boy ran ahead around the last bend, shrieking with excitement.

Even before he rounded the corner, Rocco knew which cave it was. He knew it just by the feel of the place, the sudden drop of the precipice, the desert beyond, and the moaning of the wind. And when he stood there in front of the cave, saw the same fire and the same iron pot and the same pile of straw and furs in the far end, a chill went through him, and he felt only the rough blanket about his nakedness, and the cold wet mouth of the wolf.

Imma saw his face, and made the children go to the back of the cave, and sit quietly on the furs there. She took two pottery bowls from the bench carved into the cave wall, and filled them with warm stew from the pot. She gave them to the children to share, to keep them occupied. Then she went back to Rocco, and watched him anxiously.

For a long time he stood looking into the cave, saying nothing. His lips were white, and he hardly breathed. He went in after a while, and went to the earth bench and touched the bowls and knives spread out there. He picked up one of the bowls, and ran his dusty finger down a long crack in the side. He put it down again, carefully, and passed his hands over his face. His fingers were shaking. Reality and dream rushed into one, confusing and terrifying him. He felt as if something powerful and significant had happened here — or would happen — and the awesomeness of it overwhelmed him. Finally he calmed down, and looked behind him at the bed of furs. The children grinned back at him, stew dribbling down their chins.

"Do you be all right, Rocco?" asked Imma gently.

Rocco met her wide, frightened eyes, and smiled. "I be fine," he replied. "Where's Ayoshe?"

"Gone," said Wyll, from the cave entrance. "She's hunting, maybe, or gone to the spring further on for water."

Imma began wandering around the cave, examining Ayoshe's belongings. "She has many things we don't," she said, fingering a fine woven garment carefully folded in an alcove in the wall. "She has jars of seeds, and fine clothes, blankets, and metal sewing things. She traded a long time before we came. She . . . don't touch that, Rocco!"

Rocco had discovered a tiny shelf carved deep into the cave wall, and the soft red leather bag, containing something heavy. He had taken the bag down, and was about to open it.

"No!" Imma's face had gone white, her whole body rigid with fear. "Don't touch those! No one touches Ayoshe's Knowing-Stones. No one. Not ever."

Rocco looked at the bag in his hands, then back at Imma's face. He replaced the bag, carefully. "What are Knowing-Stones?" he asked.

"They be her sacred symbols," said Imma quietly. "She uses them to guide us, to help us decide big things, and to tell us the meanings of our dreams. No one touches them, except she offers. They be only for ones who need to know."

"I'm a perfect candidate," muttered Rocco, turning away. He wiped his hands on his trousers, as if something from the sacred stones still clung to them. He noticed some drawings scratched into the cave wall, and went over to them.

He stood looking at them, bewildered. The drawings were clear and precise, and strangely symmetrical. There were straight lines and spheres, planet shapes and flames, and strange conical forms that reminded Rocco vaguely of spacecraft. The drawings were formal, mathematical, and out of character with everything in the cave — with everything in Anshur. They amazed Rocco, and puzzled him deeply.

Tisha stood beside him, swinging on his arm,

and looked at the drawings with him. "They be dragons," she said.

"No, they're not," said Rocco. "I've seen dragons. They're nothing like that."

"They do be dragons," said Imma quietly, from behind him. "They breathe arrows of fire, and they fly in the air. I know. Ayoshe told me."

"Well, Ayoshe doesn't know what dragons are, either," said Rocco.

"You think you know all things, don't you?" said Imma, with a bitter little smile. "Well, you don't. Ayoshe knows more than you."

She took the pottery bowls from the children, and placed them back on the shelf. She shepherded the children out, making sure that Tisha was holding Morg's hand. She headed them back down the path towards the ridge. "We'll see you in the valley," she called back to Rocco. "You wait for Ayoshe. She'll tell you they're dragons."

Rocco waited until they were gone. He collected some dried dung from the pile outside the cave entrance, and threw it on the dying fire. When the flames were roaring again, he went to the small shelf holding the Knowing-Stones, and looked at it. For a long time he stood there, deciding. Then, slowly, he took the bag down.

Six

There were twelve Knowing-Stones, each flat and roughly oval, and small enough to hold comfortably in one hand. Rocco spread them out on the dust in a patch of sunshine in the cave's entrance. He liked the texture of them, liked their cool, smooth surfaces and the strange, beautiful drawings etched onto them.

There was a stone with a picture of a sheaf of wheat, another with a bird, and one with a primitive plough. There was an arrow, a cup, a rising sun, a figure like a number eight, and a pair of human eyes. There were scales balancing, a cross, an ancient tower, and a tent. Rocco picked up the stone with the tent, turning it over in his hands, smoothing the etching with his fingers. The stone felt good in his hands, and seemed to have a power, a weightiness that disturbed and fascinated him. He could believe the stones were sacred: He would not believe they were harmful.

He examined them all, wondering what their

symbols meant. Always he returned to the stone with the picture of the tent, drawn to it as certainly as if it had been engraved with his name. He turned all the stones upside down and moved them around in the dust, even burying some. Then he closed his eyes and moved his fingers among the stones, choosing one blindly. Even before he turned it over and opened his eyes, he knew which stone it was. The tent. The dwelling in the desert.

Unnerved, he put all the stones back in the bag, blowing the dust off them first, and pulled the drawstring closed. He put the bag back in its place, and brushed the dust from his hands. He took down a bowl, got himself some broth from the stew in the pot, and sat on the furs to drink it. It tasted of rosemary and thyme, and was delicious.

For a long time he sat there, waiting. The air grew cold, and he wished he'd worn his sheepskin jacket after all. He listened to the awesome silence of the mountains, and felt as if he were the only person in all the world. Yet he was not lonely: The presence of Ayoshe filled the cave like incense, and her touch was on everything, even him.

Rocco decided to go. He put his bowl on the ground near the cave entrance, and took his knife from the sheath at his waist. He wrote in the dirt by his cup: "Rocco was here. Hope you don't mind." Then he sheathed the knife, checked the fire, and left.

It occurred to him later that night that she probably couldn't read.

It was getting dark when he reached the valley. He jogged slowly to keep warm. As he passed the stone walls of the cultivated area he stopped, peering over the wall at the tidy rows of crinkled winter cabbages, almost ready, and the cauliflowers pale in the evening shadows. He smelled the rich odor of damp soil, and glanced over at the pile of huge pots used to haul water to the garden. He glanced across the flat grassland to the river, thinking. Then he ran on, smiling to himself. His new idea, if it worked, would revolutionize life in Anshur.

He came to the cliff, and noticed the huge communal fire blazing on the ground in front of the dwellings, and smelled the delicious aroma of roasting goat. Eden, the storyteller, was near the fire, turning root vegetables in the embers. She smiled and waved at Rocco, her red hair the color of the fire. He waved back, and ran on up the rough cliff steps, taking them two at a time, and on up past the other caves. He jogged along the sloping track, and covered the treacherous plank bridge in two easy strides. He swept aside the skins of his own cave entrance, and went in, panting and exhilarated.

Ilsabeth was there, combing Toukie's hair with a thick bone comb. She smiled at Rocco, and said, "You be late. It's almost time for the celebration feast."

Rocco's face went red. "Narvik's wedding-feast! I forgot."

Ilsabeth laughed. "It's a while, yet. The women be still dressing Cheyenne. Why so late?"

"I wanted to see Ayoshe."

"She's been here all afternoon," said Ilsabeth.

"He doesn't know what dragons be," giggled Toukie, tugging away from the comb. "And he touched the bag with the Knowing-Stones. He'll die tonight. I'm not sleeping next to him."

"Keep still," said Ilsabeth crossly, pulling her closer, and setting to work again with the comb. "I'll wash your hair tomorrow, Toukie, and rub lavender oil in it. You've got bugs."

"I like bugs," said Toukie.

Rocco smiled and went over to the recess in the cave wall that contained his personal belongings. He felt in the shadows for the threadbare woven cloth he used for a towel, and noticed a pale rounded object beside it. He picked it up, sniffed it, and took it over to the firelight. It was soap. There was a letter "R" carved into it, and he glanced at Ilsabeth.

"Is this from you?" he asked.

She smiled shyly. "I was making soap today. I made that one for you. It has powdered chamomile in it, for your hair."

"Thanks very much. It's lovely. Smells like apples. I didn't know you could write."

"Father showed me how today, just the first word in your name. Did I do it properly?"

"Yes. It's terrific." He smiled. "Thank you. I'll use it tonight."

"Be you going bathing now?"

"If I've time, before the feast."

"You have time," she said.

He took a clean folded shirt from the deep shelf, his one clean pair of trousers, a fur coat, and his boots. As he passed the fire on his way to the river, Petur called to him.

"Going for your wash, Rocco?" he yelled, and everyone else around the fire looked up. "You be early!" Petur went on, smiling broadly. "The women be not going down till morning."

Everyone laughed, and Rocco waved his towel at them. "I can wait," he called. Their laughter followed him along the riverbank, and he smiled as he ran. The bathing-place was downriver, opposite the garden end of the caves, and hidden around a rocky bend. There was a wide, deep pool the tribe used for washing in. It was hidden from view of the dwellings, and totally protected from the wind. On this side of the river the dark cliff walls rose all around, towering almost vertically. On the other side the mountains tumbled down to the river's edge, making a rocky barrier between the river and the western Voidances. Already the sun had slipped behind the peaks, and the water was icy cold.

The bathing hole was the only truly safe swimming place in the whole river, being bordered all around by a circle of smooth high rocks. Even small children could swim here in relative safety, as long as they stayed within the circle of stones. Outside the pool, the current was so strong even Rocco had difficulty swimming against it.

At the base of the shadowy cliff he stripped, dropping his clothes on the ground. He left his clean clothes spread out on a rock, ready to get into as soon as he was dry again. He ran down to the pool, his soap clutched tightly in his hand,

and dived into the deep black waters. He came up gasping. He scrubbed his hair quickly, and washed the grime from his hands and feet. He soaped himself all over, got out and placed the soap carefully on the shore, and then ran back in to rinse off, yelling. His shouts echoed off the shadowy cliffs all around, sounding hollow and weird.

He crouched in the river, his chin just above the water, and called, slowly and solemnly, "Rocco calling the twentieth century. Anyone there?"

The words resounded off the high rock walls, filling the gorge with somber echoes.

"Rocco calling the twentieth century," he called again, in deep tones. "Any telegrams for Rocco?"

He listened to the echoes, grinning. Then came a reply, gloomy and deep: "No telegrams for Rocco. Sorry."

Rocco shot upright in the water, rigid with terror. His heart leapt madly in his ribs, and he thought he was going to pass out. Then he heard a laugh, and saw a shadow move up by the cliffs.

"Narvik!" he choked, and felt his knees turn weak. "Narvik, you stupid idiot!" He climbed out of the water, shivering, and Narvik came down to meet him, bringing the towel. Rocco took it, and swore. "You gave me the fright of my life," he growled.

Narvik laughed softly and bent to pick up the soap. "What's a telegram, Rocco?"

"A letter. A written message." Rocco shook uncontrollably as he dried himself, and dropped the towel several times. His lips were blue, and his skin felt like a plucked chicken. The thin cloth of the towel was soaked in seconds, and useless. He hopped and leapt up the stones, stubbing his toes in the darkness, and pulled on his clean clothes. He wondered whether anyone had hidden cockroaches up his trouser legs, then remembered he was with Narvik and not the kids. Narvik's sense of humor was slightly more sophisticated.

"Who were you calling?" Narvik asked, as Rocco dried his feet and dragged on his boots. "Were you calling your god?"

"No. I was calling my tribe," said Rocco sheepishly. "Acting the goat. I wasn't serious."

They began walking back again. "You miss your tribe?" asked Narvik gently.

Rocco thought about it for a while, carefully negotiating the sharp stones in the dark. "No. Not really," he said at last. "I like it here, Narvik. Life's good. It's hard, but good. There's something whole and clean about gathering herbs, growing your own vegetables, washing in the river, and killing your own meat and cooking it over a fire. I like this kind of life. It means something." He glanced sideways into Narvik's face, and asked suddenly: "What are you doing here, anyway? It's your wedding-feast tonight. Why aren't you getting ready? You're supposed to be the nervous groom."

"I be ready now," said Narvik, with a slow smile. "I needed peace, Rocco. They be taunting me back at the caves, without mercy."

"I know. They never let up," grinned Rocco.

"They still tease me about the time I went bathing with the women. Are you nervous?"

Narvik smiled, and shrugged. "In a way. It's one thing to take Cheyenne in the forest, when we be both alone and laughing and joying one another. It's another thing to take her in our own new cave, with all the tribe knowing, and joking in the morning."

"My tribe has all that worked out," said Rocco. "When two people marry, they go away for a time alone together. It's called a honeymoon."

"Your tribe is wise, in certain ways," commented Narvik. "Do our ways be very different from your own?"

"Yes. Most people in my tribe wouldn't last a day out here."

"You did."

"I was fit. And it was still hard."

"The children be tough teachers," said Narvik gravely. "My father said, if you could survive five days with them, you could survive anything."

"I see," muttered Rocco, with a small smile. "And do all new recruits get beaten into line by the kids?"

"Your saying is hard. Recruits?"

"Newcomers to the tribe."

"There be no newcomers. Traders come and go, but no one has been allowed to stay before."

"Then why me?"

Narvik shrugged. "Because Ayoshe said."

"And no one argued with her," said Rocco. "She made a decision about me that overruled everything, and she hadn't even met me. I'd give a million dollars to know what's in her head."

"What's a million dollars?" asked Narvik.

"Ah. . . . A huge herd of goats, enough clothes for forty tribes, and ten caves piled high with fine bows. And then more."

Narvik gave a low whistle. "You must come from a wealthy tribe, Rocco."

They rounded the last riverbend, and saw before them the dark, beautiful valley, the cliff dwellings pink in the sunset glow, and the fire blazing. The smell of smoke and roast meat was tantalizing on the night wind, and they could hear the children playing games and singing while they waited for dinner. Rocco looked across at Narvik, and slowly shook his head.

"My tribe isn't rich, Narvik," he said sadly. "It isn't rich at all."

Ilsabeth came around the fire and sat close to Rocco. "Hold out your hand," she said, and trickled golden grain into his palm.

"What's this for?" he whispered.

"When the ceremony is over, we throw the grain over Narvik and Cheyenne," she whispered back. "It is for fertility."

Rocco nodded and looked at Narvik and Cheyenne. They stood together in front of the fire, waiting for Ayoshe to begin the ceremony. They each wore a beautiful full-length garment dyed deep red, and a long cloak of pure white fur. Over their hair they each wore a garland woven of rosemary and wheat. Narvik looked flushed and tense, his eyes solemn and dark. His sixteen-year-old bride, tall almost as himself, was smiling and calm. The garland of wheat mingled with the flaming gold of her hair, alive and rich in the fire's light. She slipped her hand into Narvik's, and whispered something to him that made him smile and relax.

From one of the caves above someone began playing a tune on a group of wind chimes. The notes rang out joyous and deep into the evening air, and were joined by the pure, primitive tones of someone playing reed pipes. The music rose in the wind, wild and joyful, and then Ayoshe came and took her place before the young people to be married, facing them and the fire, with all the tribe gathered quietly behind her. Everyone sat, except Ayoshe and the bride and groom.

The music slowly died, until the only sounds were the crackling of the fire and the scream of a wildcat far in the mountains. For a while Ayoshe said nothing. Then she placed a hand on Narvik's shoulder, and one on Cheyenne's, and bent her head.

When she spoke, her voice was quiet and crystal clear. "Our beloved God," she said, "bless Narvik and Cheyenne. Bless their dreams, their bodies, and their love. Give them strength in the hard times, peace in the bad times, and joy in each other always. Let their cave be a dwelling-place of love."

She lowered her arms, and sat on the ground. They knelt in front of her, their heads close. The fire leapt and sparked behind them, casting long black shadows across the shining dust towards the watching tribe. Rocco saw Ayoshe take a dark bag that was tied to her belt, and she spread something on the ground.

He glanced at Ilsabeth. "What's happening now?" he whispered.

"Ayoshe is using her Knowing-Stones. Narvik and Cheyenne will tell her of their most powerful dreams, and each choose a Knowing-Stone. She will tell them what their dreams do mean, and the meanings of the stones they choose."

"What if the meanings are bad?"

"Then she will tell them gently, and give them courage to walk where they must walk," she said.

"Is it all true? Do the Knowing-Stones really work?"

"Rocco." Her voice was full of reproach, but her lips were curved. "Ayoshe does never lie, neither do her stones."

The wind chimes were being played again, softly, and the pipes with them. The music was earthy, beautiful and powerful. Rocco listened, feeling unbearably happy, and at the same time unaccountably sad. The music was all pleasure and pain, joy and sorrow, triumph and despair, and it moved him to tears. He felt Ilsabeth's hand warm and light on his thigh, and he placed his own hand over hers and held it there.

After a while the music stopped, and Ayoshe and the young couple stood up again. Narvik and Cheyenne faced each other, their hands pressed palm to palm. Together they spoke their vow: "I pledge you my body, my love, my life."

Then Ayoshe lifted her arms to the starry skies, and prayed the last wedding prayer.

"God of our life," she prayed, "let these two

be made one. Let their spirits be united always, for as long as they walk this earth."

She lowered her arms and took the hands of the bride and groom, and said with deep joy: "I name you wife and husband. I bless you, in the name of Mother-Father God. Go in peace."

She released their hands, and Narvik put his arms around Cheyenne and kissed her.

Rocco looked at Ilsabeth, and saw that she was watching him, her eyes wide and luminous in the fire's light. Her lips were slightly parted. She looked tender and vulnerable, and for the first time he didn't feel inferior to her.

"Will you ever go away, Rocco?" she asked, in a whisper.

He bent his head and didn't answer. Softly, she moved her hand until her palm was uppermost, her fingers interlaced with his. "Will you?" she asked again.

"I don't know," he murmured.

"If your tribe called for you, would you go?"

"Yes."

She pulled her hand free then, and stood. Everyone was standing, flinging handfuls of grain across the wedding pair. The wheat glittered like golden rain in the firelight. The pipes were playing again, a mad joyous tune, and everyone was laughing and hugging. Rocco remembered to throw his grain, missed Narvik and his wife, and showered Imma instead. She laughed, and blew him a kiss. Tisha ran up to Rocco and flung her arms around his waist. "We be going to eat till we bust!" she cried, her eyes shining. "Will you sit with me?"

"Don't I, always?" he said, smiling. He pushed

his way through the noisy crowd and congratulated Narvik. He was going to shake Narvik's hand, but Narvik caught him up in a hug that knocked the breath out of him and, laughing, swept the garland of wheat off his own head and placed it crookedly on Rocco's. He whispered something Rocco didn't hear. Then Petur was there to congratulate his son and greet his new daughter, and Rocco stepped aside, almost knocking over Jakob. Jakob saw the crown of wheat, and frowned.

"You be getting all the best of everyone's, Rocco," he said darkly. "But you be coming to the end of it."

"What do you mean?" asked Rocco, but Jakob was already leaning towards Cheyenne, and giving her a hard and unbrotherly kiss. Rocco glared at Jakob's back and walked away.

"What's the matter?" asked Tisha, skipping along beside him, and kicking up clouds of firelit dust and grain. "Do you be angry, Rocco?"

"No." He bent suddenly and picked her up, swinging her across his back, and galloped off to the clean straw and pottery bowls spread out across the ground. "Let's help carve up the meat, Tisha. I'm starving."

Petur sat down heavily on the ground beside Rocco, groaned, and belched. "It is a fine and mighty wedding-feast, is it not?" he said.

"Fantastic," agreed Rocco, wiping dark juice off his chin with his hand. "I didn't think you people ate like this. It's like Christmas."

"And what is this Christmas thing?" asked

Petur. He added quickly, "Don't answer."

Ayoshe was sitting down on Rocco's other side, setting her empty bowl on the ground in front of her. She looked at the garland of wheat sitting crookedly on Rocco's hair, and chuckled. "I see you've settled in well here," she observed.

Rocco nodded and smiled back, wondering what was so amusing. "It was a nice wedding service," he said. "I liked your prayers."

"Thank you. And thank you for your message."

"My message?" Rocco stuffed another fried cricket into his mouth, and gave her a bewildered look. "What message?"

"In the dust outside my cave. I didn't mind your being there at all. My home is yours."

"Thanks. You can read, then?"

Ayoshe fought to keep her face straight. "A little."

Petur chuckled richly. "Ayoshe can do everything," he said. "She even shoots an arrow better than I do."

"Talking of arrows," said Rocco, with his mouth full, "when can I have a bow, and practise?"

"When Jakob teaches you," said Petur. "Tomorrow."

"Can I practise a bit by myself first?"

"There is no purpose, Rocco. A bow is a lethal weapon. You will learn properly, with Jakob."

Rocco knew better than to argue. He glanced at Ayoshe, willing her to support his request, but she said nothing. He sighed, disappointed, and finished his meal. The wooden hunting bows used here were very different from his own fiberglass bow at home. He had hoped to be reasonably skilled with the new one before he shot in front of Jakob. Then he remembered something else.

"I've had an idea that might help your tribe, Petur," he said. "I've thought of a simple irrigation system, to lift water from the river and take it in clay pipes to your garden. It'd save hauling water all that way in those heavy pots. It'd be quicker, too, and more efficient. And effortless, once it's going."

Petur leaned forward, interested. He was picking his teeth with a sliver of bone. "Speak on," he said.

"I saw something like it in a book once," went on Rocco, eager and excited. "It's a large wheel fixed with scoops for the water. It's placed in the river, and when it's turned, the scoops fill and lift the water to the riverbank, where they tip it into a channel. The channel takes the water to the garden. I'll draw a picture of it in the morning, it'll be clearer. But all you need is a big wheel, the scoops for the water, and the pipes. We could make the scoops and the pipes out of clay and bake them in the kiln."

"We have a wheel," said Petur, rubbing his beard. "It is stored in the cave with the weapons and the grain. It came from a trader's cart, a long time past."

"Then it wouldn't be hard to make," said Rocco.

Petur nodded slowly, impressed, and put a hand on Rocco's shoulder. "Draw it for me in the morning," he said. "If this thing works, it will change our lives."

Rocco nodded and placed his empty bowl on the ground beside Ayoshe's. In a few seconds Tisha was there, picking both bowls up. "I be washing them," she said, licking the rim of Rocco's.

"Take them to the river, my love, and do it properly," said Ayoshe. "Ask one of the older girls to help."

"I be old enough," said Tisha, but caught the look in Ayoshe's face, and ran off to find Imma.

Rocco pushed the garland of wheat back off his forehead, and watched the young people dancing on the edge of the firelight. The music was rich, rhythmic, and seemed at times almost familiar. The dances were like folk dances, with steps worked out in various patterns, complicated turns, and clapping at set intervals.

"Our dances be not difficult to learn," said Petur, watching Rocco's face. "Would you like to try?"

Rocco was up like a shot, and on his way to find Ilsabeth, when Ayoshe called him back. "I have a word for you," she said.

Rocco was already dancing backwards away, and several people were watching him, laughing and applauding. "Tell me later," he said to Ayoshe. "After the dance."

"It is a word for now," she called urgently.

"What?" He shook his head, grinned, and waved at her. He turned and went over to Ilsabeth. She was sitting talking to Wyll. "Will you come and dance with me, Ilsabeth?" he asked.

She looked at the golden wheat blazing across his dark hair, and her cheeks went scarlet. "Do you be sure, Rocco?"

"Of course I be sure. I'd like to dance with you."

She got up, hesitant but graceful, and he took her hand and led her over to the group of dancers. The musicians were standing nearby. Two men were playing reed pipes, and another beat a drum. A woman played an instrument similar to a xylophone, but made of wood, and sounding deeper-toned, and rich. Someone else played a harp.

"You'll have to teach me the steps," said Rocco, and Ilsabeth smiled shyly and took his hand. The other dancers watched while she showed him, clapping and cheering. When Rocco had mastered the routines, they all joined in.

The dance was interrupted by a loud cheer, and much laughter and clapping, and Rocco looked up to see Narvik taking Cheyenne up the cliff steps to the cave he had prepared for her. Ayoshe went with them, and stayed a long time. Several dances later, when Ayoshe still had not returned, Rocco asked Ilsabeth what she was doing there.

"She's giving Cheyenne the herbs, and talking," said Ilsabeth.

"What herbs?"

"To bring on a woman's special time, and prevent babies until they be wanted," she explained. "And she's instructing Narvik, making sure he's wise in all things."

"It's a bit late for that," murmured Rocco. "He's already wise."

"Be you mocking our ways?" she asked defensively, half smiling.

"Never. I admire your openness and honesty. It makes a refreshing change."

She looked bewildered, and he smiled and pulled her closer, and they danced in silence, following in the steps of the other dancers, their hands held.

The night deepened, and the wind blew in cold along the valley, and more fuel was thrown on the fire. Rocco danced with all the women, and even danced with Tisha, to her joy. He danced with Ayoshe when she came back, and astonished everyone. Someone told him later that Ayoshe had never danced, not in all her years in the valley. Rocco felt privileged, and humbly pleased. But always he returned to Ilsabeth, and danced with her.

The fire died low again, the night gathered in, and the younger children yawned and were taken away to bed. Only a few people remained dancing, their pale clothes glowing apricot in the fire's last light. Rocco guided Ilsabeth into the night beyond the fire. He closed his hands about her neck gently, and drew her close to him.

She pulled away, confused. "This is not dancing," she said.

"It is, in my tribe."

"This close?"

"Even closer," he murmured, "though I'd better not, with your father watching."

"You do lie, Rocco." She laughed softly, and he drew her close again and kissed her forehead, nose, and lips. She turned her face aside, but he felt her arms slip around his waist. He kissed the smooth line of her jaw, and her throat. She made a small moaning sound, and turned her mouth to his.

There was a commotion over by the river, and desperate shouts. Rocco groaned and tried to ignore them, but Ilsabeth pulled free, and started to run. Someone rushed past Rocco from the direction of the river. He glimpsed the sleek shine of a bow, and heard an urgent shout.

"Petur! Wildcat! One goat, gone."

Rocco followed, and joined the group gathering near the fire. Someone had thrown on more fuel, and the flames leapt across tense, white faces. Petur had his hands on the shoulders of the youth with the bow, calming him. "Tell me what happened, Dayv," he said quietly.

"Wildcat," panted the youth. Sweat was pouring down his face, and blood dripped down his right sleeve. His coat was torn, the sleeve ripped almost off. "I never heard it come. It were too close at first to shoot. I tried to save the goat. I be sorry."

"It's all right," said Petur gently. "You were alone to shepherd them, while we feasted. There is no blame. And you be wounded."

"I shot the cat as it ran, wounded it in the shoulder. It were already lame, and were after easy prey."

Petur beckoned to Jakob. "You watch the goats until morning. Hurry. They be unguarded." Jakob ran off towards the caves, and Petur shouted after him: "Bring a spear for Rocco, and the poisoned arrows."

Rocco waited, shivering in the tense silence.

The youth who had been guarding the goats sank to the ground, and someone helped him off with his coat. The shirtsleeve underneath was soaked in blood.

"Has Ayoshe gone?" asked Petur, peering into the darkness.

"She went, long past," said Eden. "Ilsabeth is getting medicines."

Rocco suddenly realized he'd need a warmer coat, if he was going to help Jakob guard the goats. He ran to the cliff and hurried up the dim paths, keeping close to the fire-reddened walls, and entered his own cave.

Ilsabeth was sorting through some dried herbs she kept in several pottery jars, collecting some into a leather pouch. The fire was nearly out, but she had lit a small clay lamp, and Rocco could smell the fat burning. He hurried over to his shelf, and fumbled in the dark for his heavy coat. He found it and pulled it on, then took off the garland of wheat and tossed it on the bed.

"Where's Jakob?" he asked.

"Gone to the weapons cave, to get a spear for you, and the poisoned arrows," she replied. She was gathering up narrow strips of soft leather, to be used as bandages. As he was about to go, she called him back.

"Rocco?"

"What is it?"

She hesitated. "Be careful."

"I will." He smiled. "I'm not scared of cats, even wild ones."

"It's not the cat that worries me," she said. "It's Jakob."

Seven

Petur stood by the rope bridge and watched Jakob go across. His hand was on Rocco's shoulder, detaining him. "I want a word with you, Rocco," Petur said. "I know things be not good between you and Jakob. But he is the best teacher you can have, our best tracker, our best bowman. You'll be guarding the goats now, not hunting; but whatever he tells you to do, you do, immediately and without question. Do you understand?"

Rocco nodded and stepped onto the bridge, gripping the rope sides. It was a precarious crossing, but he was used to it by now. Below him, the shallow water rushed black and gurgling, and he thought of the time Imma and the children dragged him through it, unconscious. It seemed a hundred years ago. He reached the stony ground on the other side, and Jakob handed him his spear. "Don't put it down till we be back at the caves," Jakob growled. He strode ahead, and Rocco hurried alongside, stumbling often on the rough ground. There was a full moon, and every rock and blade of grass was edged in silver-blue.

They climbed up to the low hills where the grass grew thick, and found the goats scattered not far from the forest. The animals were nervous, and difficult to herd together again. Rocco noticed that Jakob had collected a pile of small stones from the riverbank, putting them into a leather pouch at his waist, and he used those to keep the goats in order, aiming them accurately and fast.

When the goats were under control, Rocco sat on a low rock, his spear across his knees. Jakob paced the coarse grass, his eyes on the goats, the moonlit mountain slopes, and the forest. Rocco noticed that he was never at any time relaxed.

"Do you think it will come back?" Rocco asked.

"Not tonight," said Jakob. "Only wolves, tonight."

Rocco shivered. He feared wolves more than anything else in Anshur. He swallowed nervously, and his fingers tightened around his spear.

"You know how to use that?" asked Jakob.

"Imma taught me," replied Rocco. "We speared fish, sometimes."

"They be different from wolves," said Jakob, with a hard laugh. "Do you think you be able to kill a wolf?"

"I'd kill anything, if it was trying to kill me," said Rocco.

They fell silent, and Jakob sat on a rock near Rocco's, his bow held lightly. His body was tense, his eyes alert to everything that moved.

"Remember what you said to me at the feast?" asked Rocco. "When Narvik gave me the wheat?"

Jakob nodded, his face grim.

"What did you mean?" asked Rocco. "Was the garland something special?"

Jakob glared at him, his strange eyes full of anger and contempt. "You truly don't know?" he asked harshly.

"No. Narvik said something, but I didn't hear it."

Jakob watched the goats again. "Then you have wronged my sister," he said softly, with venom. "You go back on your word now, Rocco, and I'll kill you."

Rocco said nothing, while there settled across him the awful realization that he had taken part in a custom about which he knew nothing.

"You accepted the wedding-garland," said Jakob. "If you didn't want it, you should have passed it on." One of the goats strayed, and without stopping in his speech, Jakob took a stone from his pouch and aimed it expertly at the ground directly in front of the goat. It shied back, and returned to the herd. "But you kept it," went on Jakob, "and you danced with Ilsabeth. He who keeps the garland is pledged to the first girl he dances with."

Rocco swore and stood up. "Why didn't you tell me?" he shouted. "I didn't know about your stupid custom! Nobody told me."

"Sit down, stop shouting. You be disturbing the goats."

Rocco did as he was told, and lowered his voice. "I can't be held responsible for this," he hissed. "I didn't know."

"You expect us to change our ways just because you don't know?"

"You don't have to change anything. Nothing's happened."

"Tell that to Ilsabeth. Yesterday she were alone. Now, she is promised."

"What do you mean, promised? She never said anything."

"She agreed to dance with you. That was her acceptance."

"Hell, I was asking her to dance with me, not marry me! How can I be married? I haven't left school yet!"

"You can be under promise for two summers. Then you marry."

"I won't be here in two summers."

"Then you break your word, and wrong my sister."

"I never promised her anything. I didn't know, Jakob. She'll understand. I'll talk to her. She knows I'm new to all this."

"She knows you wore the wedding-garland, and asked her to dance."

There was a sound from the forest behind them, and Rocco felt the hair rise along the back of his neck. It was a long hollow howl from a wolf. In an instant Jakob was on his feet, his bow drawn and an arrow in place. Rocco hadn't even seen his hand reach for the quiver, he had moved so fast.

"There is only one, I think," murmured Jakob,

lowering the bow. "I'll stay and guard the goats. You go and frighten off the wolf."

Rocco gave a short laugh, and sat down again.

"I said, go!" said Jakob angrily.

Rocco looked at him, and for a moment their eyes locked. Jakob's teeth glimmered in the moonlight. "Be you afraid, Rocco?"

Rocco stood up then, gripped his spear until his knuckles were white, and turned and walked down the hillside to the forest. It was almost dawn now, and the ground was lit with a cold grey light. The skies to his right, beyond the cliff dwellings and Ayoshe's mountain, were flushed with pink. The forest ahead was pitch-black. Rocco went on, never faltering in his stride.

The ground was smoother here, the grass thicker. As he neared the forest, Rocco smelled the spruce trees, and the pungent odor of mosses and lichen on the damp forest floor. The wolf howled again, and Rocco stopped. He was only five meters from the first trees. He walked on again, silent and cautious, his spear held in readiness. He hoped Jakob was behind him with the bow, but nothing on earth would have made him look back.

He went on, entered the shadows under the trees, and felt the mosses soft beneath his feet. He could hardly breathe. He walked on, softly, listening. A branch cracked, and he nearly dropped his spear. He froze, listening. He began to move again, straining his eyes in the gloom. He could barely make out the shapes of the trees. Then something moved, and he saw the wolf.

It was only a few meters away. It was large

and grey, and its green eyes burned on him. It didn't move, just stood there, watching.

Frighten it off, Jakob had said. Just like that. Frighten it off.

The wolf took a step forward. Without thinking, Rocco screamed at it and waved his arms, rushing forward and slashing with the spear. Insects flew all around; the forest leapt to life, echoing, and the wolf turned and fled. In three seconds, it was all over.

Shaking uncontrollably, and breathing as if he'd run a marathon, Rocco looked at the empty space where the wolf had been. He gave a short, nervous laugh and started to walk back, glancing every now and again over his shoulder. He started to run out of the forest and didn't stop until he neared the place where Jakob sat. He changed his run to an easy jog, reached the rock and sat down calmly, his spear across his knees.

"I heard a lot of noise," said Jakob. "What happened?"

"I killed it," said Rocco smoothly.

"There is no blood on your spear."

"No. I strangled it with my hands. We do that for sport, in my tribe."

Jakob stood up and faced Rocco, looking at him sharply, wavering between doubt and admiration. A muscle twitched at the corner of Rocco's mouth, and Jakob sat down again. "Liar," he said, without rancor.

They sat in silence, while the skies lightened and turned pink, and the misty mountains blushed. Rocco slumped forward, dozing. He woke up when Jakob spoke.

"When be you going, Rocco?"

"Going?" Rocco jerked upright. He rubbed his hands across his face, and pressed his fingers to his bleary eyes. "Who's going?"

"You, before two summers pass." Jakob was standing a little way apart, skinning a rabbit he had shot. Rocco realized he must have been asleep for a while, and shame swept over him. He stood up and stamped around to wake himself. He was frozen, and his breath made mist on the morning air.

"I don't know when I'm going," he said, "but I am going."

"Will traders from your place call for you?"

"No. But if other traders come, I might go with them." He watched Jakob finish his task, cleanly and expertly. "What country is this?" Rocco asked.

"Country?" Jakob wiped his knife on the grass, and sheathed it. He stood up and placed the rabbit's carcass and the pelt on a rock, away from insects in the grass. "That saying is hard, Rocco."

"Country. You know. Finland, Alaska, Norway. Where are we?"

Jakob looked blank, and shook his head. "We be in the Valley of Anshur," he said.

Rocco sighed and went for a short walk. He looked across the river at the dwellings in the cliff, purple with shadows. The sky behind them was brilliant. He watched the sunrise, his arms crossed for warmth, his hands buried deep in the fur of his coat. Again, he was struck with the wild beauty of Anshur, its unspoiled grandeur and peace. His eyes returned to the caves, to the dark skins covering the entrance to his home. He saw a movement on the cliff, and a figure crept along the sloping path to the ground, passed the remains of the fire, and went on around the riverbend towards the toilet pit.

Another figure left the cliff and came this way across the bridge. It was Jaim, Eden's son, who had given Rocco extra clothes. He climbed the slope to Rocco, smiling broadly, and handed him a round thick oatcake and a slice of pale goats' cheese. Rocco accepted the meal, though he wasn't hungry. People here didn't usually eat breakfast; they had only a light midday meal in their own caves, and the shared feast at night.

"Any trouble last night?" Jaim asked, and Rocco shook his head.

"Does Father want us to stay here all the day?" asked Jakob, eating his food with relish.

"No," Jaim replied. "You be expected back at the caves now. I'm to shepherd the herd. I'll use Rocco's spear." He picked it up from where it leaned against a rock, and Rocco remembered he had been told not to put it down. Again, he felt ashamed. He hadn't done too well, this first learning time with Jakob. But Jakob said nothing, just finished his oatcake and cheese, picked up the rabbit and pelt, and began walking down the hill.

Rocco followed after him, jogging in long easy strides. The sun was fully risen now, and the day shone. He ran all the way to the river, and knelt on the stones to drink.

Jakob knelt beside him and drank too, then

they rested back on their heels and looked across at the caves. There were people all up and down the paths now, and smoke wafted from rekindled fires behind the skins. Children wailed, grumpy after their late night, and adults cajoled them, and laughed.

"Father told us a thing last night," said Jakob quietly, his eyes still on the cliff. "He said you be showing him a way to water our crops, that is better than the way we have. He thinks you be a skilled member of our tribe now."

"Not really," murmured Rocco. "I make a lot of mistakes."

"That you do," Jakob agreed bitterly. "You slept this morning. If our goats be taken, we have no milk or cheese. And you left your spear, and went for a walk. If the wolf came back, what would you do? Kill it with your hands?"

"I didn't go for a walk. I was only a few steps away."

"A few steps be all there is between life and death, sometimes."

"I'm sorry."

"You come to our valley from nowhere, and you think you know everything. You mock our ways and tell us how to change them. You walk into my father's cave and make yourself to be a son to him, and win him over with your talk and different ways. You know nothing, Rocco. Nothing."

"I said I was sorry."

"You be sorry, now? You wait till the next five days be past. You be all mine, for five days. If you forget one weapon, even blink while keeping watch, or do one foolish thing, you will know what sorry is."

Rocco fell onto the furs beside Toukie, closed his eyes, and sighed blissfully. Petur and Jakob had gone out somewhere, and only Toukie was here, curled up and snoring like a cat. Ilsabeth was at the river with the other women, bathing. Rocco was almost asleep when he heard her come back and move softly about the cave. He felt her kneel at the bottom of the bed and undo the leather cords binding up his boots. She pulled his boots off carefully, and covered him with a fur.

He smiled. "Thanks."

"Be you thirsty?" she whispered.

He shook his head, his eyes still closed. "I drank at the river."

"Jakob said you chased away a wolf."

"That was good luck, not bravery."

He felt her lie down beside him, on top of the furs, and he slipped his arm around her neck. His fingers moved in her long hair, gently.

"There's something I've got to tell you, Ilsabeth."

He felt her cool mouth on his cheek, and smelled the herbs and river water in her hair. "I'm afraid it isn't good," he added, not daring to look at her.

She sighed happily and rested her damp head on his chest. "Nothing you say to me today will touch my joy," she said. "I be singing inside, Rocco."

Toukie woke up, saw Rocco lying on his back

with his eyes closed, and Ilsabeth looking strangely misty-eyed, and she started to scream. She scrambled away from them, screaming and sobbing. "He's dead!" she howled, terrified. "He's dead!"

Rocco was with her in seconds, taking her trembling shoulders in his hands. "Toukie, look at me," he said. "I'm not dead. See?"

She screamed louder and dragged herself away, crawling to the far end of the cave, where the ceiling sloped down to the floor. She crouched there in a dark recess, whimpering.

Petur rushed in. "What's going on?" he roared. "The whole cliff do think there's been a slaughtering!"

"Rocco's dead!" wailed Toukie from her hiding place. "He touched the Knowing-Stones, and he's dead!"

Mystified, Petur looked at Rocco, and Rocco shrugged. "He looks very alive to me," he said, crouching near the back of the cave, and holding out his hand to Toukie. He coaxed her out, and made her go and stand in front of Rocco. "See? He is alive, and fine," he said gently. "Now give him a hug."

Toukie cautiously put out one hand, poked Rocco's chest, then fled to the furs and burrowed under them.

Petur stood up and looked gravely at Rocco. "Now tell me, Rocco. Did you touch the Knowing-Stones?"

"In Ayoshe's cave yesterday, with the children, I took down the bag with the stones," said Rocco evenly, meeting Petur's eyes. "I didn't know what it was. Imma told me, and I put it back."

Petur nodded, and went over to the shelf with the pottery bowls. "It is forbidden to touch her Knowing-Stones," he said. He handed Rocco and Ilsabeth each a drink, and got one for himself. He sat by the fire, and smiled at them. "Sit down," he said. "I drink to both of you." He held his bowl high. "To your lives," he said, and drank.

Rocco glanced at Ilsabeth, standing quiet and smiling beside him, and felt trapped. He knew now was the time, but his tongue wouldn't move. The skins in the doorway opened, and Jakob came in, with Narvik and Cheyenne.

"Welcome, my wedding children!" cried Petur, leaping to his feet. He embraced his son and new daughter, and got them each a drink of the herb tea. He gave one to Jakob as well. "Sit down by my fire," he said, cheerfully. "We have much today to be glad for."

"We have a wounded wildcat to be decided on," murmured Jakob, sitting across the fire from Rocco. "And a fool who needs to speak."

No one heard him. Narvik sat down near Rocco, and gave him a friendly punch and a broad grin. "I hear you kept the wedding-garland," he said. "You cunning fox, Rocco. You be quick to decide, in your tribe."

Rocco looked at the flames and tried to smile. Ilsabeth sat on his other side, and smiled shyly across at Narvik and Cheyenne. "He did dance with me," she said.

"That too we heard," said Cheyenne. "You be pleased, my new father?"

Petur's smile widened. "I be pleased."

Rocco glanced up and saw Jakob's tawny eyes boring into him. He swallowed nervously, and his hands tightened about his bowl. He opened his mouth to speak, but Narvik said, "I heard that a wildcat last night took one of our goats."

"Yes." Petur's voice was heavy, his face suddenly grim. "It will have to be hunted down and killed. It's wounded, and lame. It won't be able to hunt in the mountains any more. It will hunt our goats, maybe slower prey. Our children."

"I'll go with Jakob," offered Narvik. "We'll go today."

"Not you," said Petur quickly. "You be just married, Narvik. You be freed from all dangerous hunts for twelve full moons. You know that."

"I'll go with Jakob," said Rocco.

They all looked up, surprised.

"You can't even draw a bow!" scoffed Jakob.

"I can." Rocco put down his drink, untouched, and turned to Petur. "You said that my best learning time with Jakob would be to hunt wildcat with him. I use a bow. I had my own, back with my tribe."

"You be skilled with it?"

"Yes. Your bows are longer, though, and your arrows weigh more. I'd need to practise with a new one, first."

"Very well," said Petur slowly. He looked across the fire at his younger son. "Take Rocco and find a bow and arrows that be right for him. Take him to the forest, and shoot there all day. Tonight, if you say he is good, the bow will be his, and he will hunt with you tomorrow."

Jakob got up, took his bow from the wall, picked up a light fur jerkin and his quiver, and went to where Rocco waited by the cave entrance.

"Our most powerful bows be behind the grain pots, at the back of the storage cave," said Petur. "Choose well."

Jakob lifted the skins, and Rocco went out. Jakob was about to follow when his father called him back. "Jakob — if Torun's bow is the best suited for Rocco, then Torun's it is."

Jakob's face went hard, but he nodded. He dropped the skins, and followed Rocco out.

Eight

All the way to the forest, Jakob never said a word. About twenty meters from the trees, he stopped.

"We be shooting from here," he said.

Rocco nodded, glad his bow was a powerful one. He was glad, too, there was no wind and the air was sparkling and warm. He wished he had his own bow, with its adjustable sight and stabilizers. This bow would be a new experience for him; he was going to have to shoot instinctively, relying only on his own perfect coordination of body, mind, and eye.

Jakob, watching him, gave a slow smile. "I will shoot one arrow, first," he said. "You shoot within a hand's width of my mark." Quietly, with skill and a style beautiful to watch, Jakob placed an arrow, aimed, and shot. It was perfect. The arrow bit the tree just over a meter above the ground, and in the center of the trunk.

Rocco stood still for a few moments, his left shoulder towards the tree. He placed his arrow, aimed, and drew the bow. Every move was flowing, smooth and faultless. Jakob, watching, knew that he was good, even before he shot. Rocco waited a second, his breath held, then released the arrow.

He was disappointed. It grazed the tree to the left, higher than Jakob's arrow, and dropped to the ground.

"Five more," said Jakob quietly.

Rocco breathed deeply, and relaxed. He knew what he'd done wrong; he'd been too tense, drawn the unfamiliar bow too hard, and not let go the bowstring quick and hard enough. It was going to take time to get to know this bow of Torun's. Still, he had all day.

He fitted another arrow, and tried again.

Petur handed Rocco and Jakob each a bowl of roasted meat, and sat beside them near the fire. He glanced curiously into their faces.

"Well," he said to Jakob meaningfully, "your words be welcome, when they come."

Jakob took a mouthful of meat, licked his fingers, and chewed. Petur waited, his patience growing thin. "Well?" he said again.

"He is masterful," said Jakob, and carried on eating.

"Masterful?" repeated Petur, his eyebrows raised. "That's high praise from you, Jakob."

"It's not praise at all," muttered Jakob. "It's a truth."

Ilsabeth looked at Rocco, her eyes shining. "Then you'll both hunt wildcat tomorrow," she said.

Rocco nodded, feeling suddenly tired. He'd

wanted more than anything to beat Jakob at archery. And now he had, and had only deepened the enmity between them. The victory was sweet, but it had its bitter side.

Rocco went to bed early that night, leaving everyone else listening to jokes and talking around the fire. It seemed strange, going to bed by himself. The cave seemed unusually quiet, empty and less warm. Without the constant talk, he was aware of the song of the big cave crickets high up in the black roof.

He took off all his clothes except his trousers, put them folded away, carefully brushed his feet clean, and slithered under the furs. They smelled of powdered rosemary, mint, and other herbs used to keep out insects. He sniffed, enjoying the fragrances. He lay on his back, his hands linked behind his head, and watched the fire-light play across the cave. It glimmered on the bunches of vegetables and drying herbs, and shone on his bow hanging on the wall. He saw the wedding-garland that Ilsabeth had hung above his bow, and sighed. Guilt gnawed at him. He regretted bitterly not speaking out; now the time to speak had passed, and every moment sucked him deeper into the binding of their traditions. He had hardly seen Ilsabeth since the dance, and they had spoken only a few words. Yet there was something extra between them, something compelling and pledged. He felt trapped, caught up in events and conditions beyond his control. And the terrible thing was that she was happy.

He closed his eyes, shutting out the garland,

and tried to sleep. The sounds of the feasting below had died down, and he could hear Eden's voice, strong and pure in the still night. She was telling a story. He opened his eyes, tempted to go down again and listen. He loved Eden's stories; she captured people with her voice, caught them up in her words, and sent them winging across wild new worlds, flying in the stuff that legends were made of. Her stories were better than a book, better than television, better than a movie in 3-D.

Rocco decided to stay and sleep. He lay on his side and pulled the furs up over his head. Beyond Eden's voice he could hear the wind moaning in the valley, and wildcats fighting in the hills. He didn't envy the shepherds tonight.

He slept at last, and dreamed of being jostled down a crowded street. He escaped to a supermarket, where he bought piles of packaged meat and paid for them with pots of grain. His history teacher gave him a lesson on medieval churches, then seduced him. Rocco went out and got a job as a traveling salesman, and ended up in prison for fraud. The dreams melted into each other, became frightening and confused. And through them all ran the thought of a hunt for wildcat; a line of tension in his mind, stretched and taut, like a bow at full draw.

Jakob leaned down and offered Rocco his hand. He pulled him up over the ledge, and they stood together looking across the savage terrain, breathing deeply.

"There be the tracks," murmured Jakob,

pointing with his bow along a dusty, narrow track. "They go around that bend, under the cliff. The tracks be new. We be close."

Rocco tried to control his breathing, and nodded. Sweat was dripping down his back, and his shirt stuck to him. Since dawn he and Jakob had been tracking the cat, and now the sun hung low over the opposite mountains, and the shadows were long. He looked back along the ridges they had climbed, and saw the valley like a green and golden patch of life a long, long way below. He took another drink from the leather bottle at his waist, and went on.

The wildcat tracks were obvious, in places scuffled and confused where the animal had fallen or rested.

"She is wounded badly," said Jakob, over his shoulder.

"How do you know it's a female?"

"It's a female, with cubs. Anything else would have stayed in the valley, down on easy ground, with easy prey. She do have cubs here, to come wounded all this way."

They crept along the ridge, down onto the track at the base of the cliff, and on around the corner. Suddenly the track widened to a ledge several meters wide. On the left was a precipice; on the right a low cliff with a small cave at its base. The cave was partly hidden by a low bushy shrub.

Rocco looked at Jakob. Jakob nodded, and glanced up at the top of the cliff. "I'll go up there," he whispered. "When you see me and I raise my hand, you take a stone and throw it over there, in the middle of the wide ground in front of the cave. She will come out. We both shoot, as soon as she is clear enough. There will be time for one arrow each. That is all." He started to go, then turned back. "If she comes before I be ready, she is all yours," he added with a grin.

They went back down the track a little way. Jakob took off his boots and began climbing the ridge to the top of the cliff. Rocco picked up a stone, and went back to the ledge. Without a sound he placed the stone on the ground in front of him, took a poisoned arrow from his quiver, and fitted it to the bow. Slowly, hardly breathing, he bent and picked up the stone, the bow held lightly in his left hand.

He watched the cave and the top of the cliff, his heart thundering. He saw Jakob's head, then his shoulders, then his whole body. Jakob stood with his legs spread, balancing on the edge of the cliff, on the far side of the cave. He placed an arrow on his bow, and lifted his hand. Rocco waited until Jakob's bow was aimed, then threw the stone. It landed with a dull thud, two meters in front of the cave.

Rocco lifted his bow and aimed, but didn't draw. There was a movement in the darkness of the cave; a deepening of the shadows. Then the blackness moved, and Rocco saw the cat. For a moment he faltered, confused. He'd expected a much smaller animal, a lynx maybe, or an overgrown domestic cat. This was an animal he had never seen before; a large cat with long shaggy fur, and black like a panther.

It moved out of the cave, but not far enough out to be shot. It was fine and powerful, but its coat was dull with dust, and it limped badly. Rocco drew his bow. At the same time, Jakob drew his. They waited. Three, four seconds. The cat limped forward, sniffing, tense and suspicious. It turned and faced Rocco.

There was a terrible hissing snarl, and the sliding of rubble behind him. Rocco spun around and saw a second cat. It was already in midair, already on top of him. He loosed the arrow as he hit the ground, and the cat rolled away from him, shot through its throat.

He was on his feet again, already reaching to his quiver for another arrow. There were none there. They had slipped out as he had fallen. The wounded cat was trotting towards him, swiftly. It seemed to Rocco as if, suddenly, there was no time. He became acutely aware of everything, of every movement, every glint of sunset on the dust, every line and ripple in the cat's fur. He moved backwards, felt an arrow under his foot, and bent to pick it up. He saw the cat spring, outstretched and beautiful. He saw Jakob on the cliff beyond, his bow aimed and drawn, but not loosing the arrow.

"Loose it!" Rocco screamed, but nothing happened. He felt mystified, hurt, and angry. Then the cat's huge paw came down across him, and he flung himself aside, skidding on his face in the dust to the very edge of the precipice. He heard screaming, but he didn't know whether it was Jakob's, the cat's, or his own. His mind was in chaos.

Slowly, quietness came. He lifted his head, and saw blood on the dust. His mouth was bleeding, and his nose. His right leg felt strange. He knelt up and saw blood soaking into the yellow earth. Then Jakob took his arm and helped him to stand.

Rocco saw a bloodstained smudge on the precipice beside him, and realized that the cat had gone over the edge. He peered over and saw, far below on the jagged rocks, the body of the cat. An arrow was high in its spine.

"Where's my bow?" he asked, and saw it lying on the path behind him, not far from the second animal. He picked the bow up and examined it for cracks. "It's fine," he said, smiling at Jakob. He saw Jakob looking at his leg, and glanced down. His trousers were sliced in four strips right down the thigh. A deep crimson stain was spreading through the leather, and dripping on the ground.

"I think I've ruined them," said Rocco.

Jakob just looked at him, a strange expression on his face, and Rocco turned away suddenly and was sick all over a rock. Then he felt the pain. He leaned over the rock, retching, fighting off a ridiculous impulse to sob. He was shaking so much he could hardly stand.

Jakob took off his woven shirt and sliced it into strips with his knife. He made Rocco sit down, then bandaged his leg. Then he went back to the cave. Rocco heard scuffling sounds and soft mewing. Then there was silence. He stood up and limped towards the cave. Three black cubs were lying on the ground, their throats cut.

"Did you have to do that?" Rocco asked furiously.

"What else do you suggest?" asked Jakob, coming back and picking up Rocco's bow and the scattered arrows. "That I take one home for Ilsabeth?"

"They might have lived."

"They might have," said Jakob harshly. "They might have grown up unskilled in hunting, and come down to live off us. Humans be an easy prey. Here, give me your arm."

"Aren't we taking back the pelt?" asked Rocco, looking longingly at the gleaming fur of the cat he had killed.

"I can't carry that and you," said Jakob.

"I'll walk."

"I'll throw you down the cliff, if you be difficult."

Rocco fell silent, and allowed Jakob to help him along the path and down over the ridge.

It was a slow, painful journey. Rocco didn't remember much of it afterwards; he remembered only being pushed up cliffs, dragged along ridges, and at times rolled half conscious down crumbling slopes. It became a nightmare of effort, helplessness and pain. Every step was a mammoth effort, and Jakob pushed, encouraged, supported, and goaded him. When none of that worked he abused and hit him, or carried him. And all the time a fear haunted Rocco — the horror that Jakob had deliberately loosed the arrow too late, deliberately given the wildcat a split-second chance to kill. The fear, the suspicion, rose like a knife in the pit of his stomach, and then was lost again in blackness and pain.

It was dawn when they reached the valley. The fire smoldered under the cliff, and the caves were quiet. Jakob dropped Rocco on the grass, and called out.

Nine

Rocco was in a state of shock by the time he reached his cave. He had lost a lot of blood, and was restless and deathly pale. He let Ilsabeth wash the blood and dust off his face and hands, but wouldn't let her touch the bandages. Nor would he take her advice. He paced the cave, anxious and white and suspicious. Every time she moved, he jumped. He saw her coming towards him with a bowl in her hands, and backed away.

"I'm not letting you do anything!" he shouted. "I'll cure myself."

"It's only water," she said gently. "You need to soak the bandages, and take them off so we can clean your leg."

"I'll do it." He grabbed the bowl off her, and slopped the water clumsily towards his leg. It missed, and went all over the bed. Without a word Ilsabeth filled the bowl again. She gave it to him, then picked up the wet furs and hung them over a leather cord suspended across the cave, close by the fire. She spread them there to dry, and they steamed and filled the cave with a strong leathery smell.

Ilsabeth suddenly noticed Rocco drinking the water she had given him, and she dashed the bowl from his hands, smashing it into the fire. "You be not allowed to drink!" she cried.

"I'm thirsty!" he shouted, stamping around in a pool of mud and blood.

"You've started the bleeding again," she murmured reproachfully. She knelt on the floor in front of him and gently unwound the bandages, easing them away from the clotted cuts. She used her knife to cut away the stained remains of his trouser leg. "I need to clean your cuts," she said.

"You're not touching them!" He backed away, slithering on the wet floor.

"Look at the mess you be making!" she cried. "I wish you'd lie down!"

"I'm not that stupid!" he snarled. "If I get on that bed, I know what you'll do. You'll get Narvik and Petur to hold me down while you clean out my cuts with red-hot knives. Then you'll stick maggots in them, to eat the pus. I know your filthy methods. Well, you're not using them. I'll fix myself."

"It is not good for you to be standing," she said. "You be needing blood in your head. Lie down." She tried to push him towards the bed, but he slipped in the mud and almost fell. Toukie, watching from the far side of the cave, giggled.

"Go and get some more straw from Eden's

cave," Ilsabeth told her. "Tell her we need it for our floor, since Rocco's made a river of it."

Toukie ran out, still giggling.

"You do be a pain, Rocco!" cried Ilsabeth, losing patience at last. "I'll be glad when Ayoshe is here!"

Rocco's head jerked up, and his eyes narrowed. "Ayoshe? What's she going to do?"

"Use the red-hot knives," Ilsabeth snapped, "while I get the maggots."

"You're not doing a thing!" yelled Rocco, and several little heads peered, grinning, from behind the skins in the cave entrance.

Ilsabeth picked up the bandages and dropped them in the fire. Rocco started pacing the floor, limping. He muttered to himself, feeling dizzy and sick. Ilsabeth stood near him, her hands around his arm. "You be needing help," she said softly. "Our ways in medicine be good. Nothing we do will hurt."

"Great. What are you going to do — knock me out with a club?"

"We have drugs."

"I know. You could kill off a million brain cells with the stuff you've got. I've seen it work, in poisoned arrows."

"It's not the same strength for people," she explained.

"I can fix myself. All right? Just leave me alone. I need sleep, that's all."

"You might bleed all day."

"I'll sleep outside, then."

"What be you afraid of, Rocco?"

"Afraid? Who's afraid? I've got a healthy sense of self-preservation, that's all."

The argument went on, with Rocco getting louder and more stubborn and unreasonable. They were still arguing when Ayoshe arrived.

The old woman took one look at Rocco, and noticed his white, sweating face, his shaking limbs, and the blood-streaked leg. "You're making an awful lot of noise for someone in your state," she said quietly. "I could hear you from the other end of the caves." She spread a clean skin out on the floor by the bed, and set out several pottery jars and bowls containing herbal ointments, oils, and medicines. Rocco watched, tense and suspicious.

"It is time, Rocco," Ayoshe said firmly. "Take off your trousers and lie down."

"What?" He stared, aghast. "I'm not getting undressed! I've got nothing on under these. You're not even a nurse. Neither's she."

Ayoshe stood up and put her hand on his shoulder. "Rocco," she said gravely, "I am ninety years old. There is nothing you can possibly have on your body that I haven't seen. Now get your trousers off. You're acting like a child."

Rocco wiped his face on his sleeve, and glared at Ilsabeth. Then he turned his back on her, and fumbled his way out of his trousers. He grabbed his towel from beside the furs on the drying-line, and wrapped it around his waist. He eased himself down onto the bed and stretched out his leg. He studied it, frowning. "A bit of a mess, isn't it?" he said.

Ayoshe squatted on the floor beside him, her hands already reaching for her potions. "Bring me a lamp," she said to Ilsabeth.

"What do you want fire for?" cried Rocco, trying to cover the cuts with his hands.

Ilsabeth sat down beside Ayoshe, holding the burning lamp. Rocco howled and tried to crawl away. Ayoshe gripped his arm and pulled him back. Her strength amazed him. She held a small pot of oil under his nose. "I need the lamp to see, while I clean your wounds with this," she said quietly. "It's lavender oil. Then I'm going to anoint the scratches with animal fat mixed with pounded comfrey leaves. There is also root of angelica in it, for pain, and mashed up leaves of burnet, to stop the bleeding. I shall put the ointment on with a feather, as gently as I can. Now, do you think you can withstand that agony?"

He nodded sheepishly, and lay back and relaxed. Sweat was pouring off his face, and he was shaking all over.

"Give him something for pain," Ayoshe murmured to Ilsabeth. The girl got up, and Ayoshe began cleaning Rocco's cuts. Ilsabeth came back, knelt on the furs near Rocco's head, and offered him a small bowl. He sniffed it, pulled a face, and swallowed the contents. He choked, and was almost sick. He wiped his mouth on the back of his hand, shot Ayoshe a pained and helpless look, and lay back.

The furs seemed to swallow him in vast depths as soft as summer night, and the cave expanded, became a huge glowing hall. Misty blue and green lights hung from the distant ceiling.

"Electricity," he said, licking his lips. "About time."

He felt movements on his leg, soft as butterflies, and looked down. His leg stretched away towards infinity, a vague and unfamiliar thing that wasn't part of him at all. He felt nothing, just a pleasant floating sensation, and a deep joy. A horse stood in one corner, eating hay. "Good,' he said, nodding approval. "Horses are a key factor in human development. The beginning of civilization. That one's got Julius Caesar on it. Hail, Caesar." He lifted his arm and saluted solemnly. "Greetings, noble lord. Welcome to the Valley of Anshur, bustling city of The Voidances. You can get your guys to build us a road out of here. And an airstrip. It'd do wonders for the tourist trade. And me."

Someone put a bowl near his mouth, and allowed him to drink a little. He looked sideways, expecting to see a Roman dancing girl with a goblet of wine, but it was only Ilsabeth, wearing a nurse's cap and white uniform. He sighed, disappointed, and went to sleep.

He woke at night, with the dim firelight flickering over the smoke-darkened walls. The cave didn't look right. Rocco leaned up on one elbow, frowning. They had put him in a separate bed, near the back of the cave. He could see Petur and the others under the furs, and could hear Jakob snoring. Rocco felt cold, and desperately thirsty. His leg was on fire, and felt tight and stiff. He put his hand down, and felt soft leather bandages, firmly bound. He tried to get up, but the cave spun.

"Be you all right, Rocco?" mumbled Petur, getting up.

"Yes. I'm thirsty."

"Lie still. I'll get you a drink. You be allowed one, now."

He got Rocco a drink, and Rocco took the bowl, suspiciously, sniffing it.

"Just water," smiled Petur.

Rocco drank, and handed back the bowl. "Thanks. Where's Ayoshe?"

"Gone to her cave. Ilsabeth will look after you."

Rocco lay down, his hands linked behind his head, and looked at the ceiling. Petur sat on the floor beside him, watching him carefully. "Tell me what happened today, Rocco," he said.

"What do you mean?" asked Rocco, suddenly tense. "Did I do something while I was . . ."

"When you were hunting," said Petur. "No one was injured who hunted with Jakob before. So why you?"

"I did something foolish," said Rocco slowly. "I was unprepared. There were two cats, not one. I panicked. It was my own fault."

"I think you be lying, Rocco."

"I never lie. Not often, anyway."

Petur chuckled and stood up. "You do be a good man for my tribe, Rocco. You endure, and you have courage. When it is time, I will be glad to have you as my son."

"Petur?" said Rocco. "I have to tell you something."

"In the morning," said Petur, sliding back into

his furs. "You be needing sleep, now."

Rocco's stomach churned, and he lay on his side, and tried not to think. Coward, he thought furiously. He was painfully aware of Ilsabeth, only a meter or so away. He tried not to think of her long shining hair, of her tempting eyes and lips. He tried to think of Tallulah, the beautiful Tallulah, who swam with him in the Olympic pool, and watched videos with him. Her image eluded him, and he felt frantic, lost. He tried desperately to remember her face, the color of her eyes, the way she did her hair. He couldn't. She was gone. He groaned and buried his face in the sweet-smelling straw, and wept.

Petur handed Jaim the large shoulder-blade bone he used as a spade, and climbed up onto the riverbank. "Your turn to dig," Petur said. "Dig out as far as that line of pebbles there, and make a wall straight down. Then we'll line the wall with flat stones and make a place to fix the wheel." He consulted a stiff piece of hide on which Rocco had made a charcoal drawing of the irrigation system, then strode along the riverbank and across the grassy strip to the walled garden. A kiln was built into the stone wall, its fires burning. Rocco worked on the ground nearby, his bandaged leg stretched out in front of him. He was making the clay scoops to be fixed to the wheel, in which the water would be raised. Petur knelt on one knee beside him, and watched him work.

"You be good at pottery," Petur commented, impressed.

"My father was a potter," Rocco said. "I used to help him, sometimes. How's the wall going?"

"It's hard work, but we be getting there."

"It's a perfect place for a waterwheel," said Rocco. "You'll be able to water your gardens all day, if you want, just by turning a wheel."

"Your idea is going to change our lives," said Petur. "We'll extend the garden, grow more grain for trade, and to store in case of drought. We can grow more seedling trees, replace the ones we've used, and extend the forest. We can grow many times more herbs, make more medicines to trade. With more to trade with, we can go out to the towns beyond The Voidances, and get the tools we need. I saw a fine wood-working tool, once, and never had enough to exchange for it. Now, we be able to get anything we want."

Rocco's eyebrows rose. "You'll be wanting washing machines next," he said.

Petur looked bewildered. "What?"

Rocco grinned. "Nothing."

He scrambled up, and placed his latest pottery scoop with the others he had made. He limped back, and Petur said gently, "You be not healed yet, Rocco. It is ten days since the hunt."

"I've got an infection, I think," said Rocco, not sitting down again. "I was thinking I might go and see Ayoshe."

"Ilsabeth will give you medicine."

"I know. But . . ."

Petur stood up, placed his hands on Rocco's shoulders, and gave him a searching, compassionate look. "I think it will be good for you to see our Mother," he said. "But I'll send one of

121

the children to get her. You be hardly able to walk."

"No. No, I feel like walking."

"Then let one of the children walk with you."

"I want to go alone."

"As you wish," said Petur, letting him go. "Go now, then. I'll clean up here. You have time to walk there and back, before dark."

Rocco went up to the cave and got his coat, and limped off up the valley. Petur watched him vanish between the rocks beyond the riverbend, and sighed. "You do be a stubborn, lonely son," he said sadly, "and we be losing you."

Ayoshe looked up from the meat she was carving, her queenly, ancient face creased in a welcoming smile. "Hello, Rocco. How are you?"

"Fine. May I come in?"

"You may. Sit down, warm yourself by the fire."

Rocco surveyed the cave, the clean hide spread out on the floor, set with two bowls of steaming herb tea, and a bowl of broken bread.

"I'm sorry. I've come at a wrong time," he said. "You're expecting someone."

"Only you," said Ayoshe, placing the bowl of cold meat on the hide. "Sit down, Rocco, and eat."

He gave her a quizzical sideways glance, half smiling. "And I didn't even phone," he murmured, sitting down. "This is a nice surprise. Thanks."

She brought him a bowl of water and a towel, and he washed his face and hands. They ate together in silence, comfortably, like old friends. Every so often he stole a long look at her face, marveling again at how impressive she was, how dark and knowing her eyes. She looked ageless, he thought, not ninety, or fifty, even. Sometimes she even looked young. She caught him watching her and chuckled softly.

He smiled and finished his drink. "That was good, thanks," he said. "Ayoshe, do you mind if I ask you for something?"

"Of course not."

"When I came to Anshur, I was wearing a silver chain around my neck. It had a flat piece in it, engraved with my name. My parents gave it to me. Do you know where it is?"

She got up and went over to one of the alcoves carved into her cave wall. "I have your belongings here," she said. "Do you want them all?"

"Only the chain."

She brought it to him, and he placed it around his neck. Ayoshe sat down again, her eyes on his face. He met her gaze, and saw again that strange flicker of recognition, that haunting familiarity. It was as if his face were well known to her; as if she had some unshared, private knowledge of him. The thought disturbed, tormented him.

"You've got thin, since I saw you last," Ayoshe murmured tenderly. "How is your leg?"

"I think I've got an infection in it. I get tired easily, and there's a painful lump in my groin."

"It is an infection," she murmured. "Don't look so alarmed. It's nothing my medicines won't fix. Let me see how the scars are healing."

He dragged up his trouser leg, and unwound the bandage. He pulled a face. "Horrible, isn't it?" he muttered.

"On the contrary, it's looking very good," she said. "The swelling's going down. In four days Ilsabeth can take out the sewing."

"I can't believe you did all that, and I didn't feel a thing," he said, rewinding the bandage and tying it firmly.

"You were busy holding a conference with Julius Caesar at the time," she smiled, clearing away the remains of the meal. "Are you sure you've had enough to eat?"

"Positive. I haven't eaten so much in days."

She prepared a small bowl of medicine and gave it to him. Without hesitation he drank, then handed the empty bowl back, his face twisted. "Thanks," he shuddered, "but I prefer your tea."

"It's better for you right now than tea," she said, putting the bowl on the bench with the others from the meal. "Ask Ilsabeth for some, every morning for five days. The infection will soon go. You're very lucky to be walking around, you know. Those scratches were deep. Any deeper, and you would have had tendons cut, and been lamed. And if Jakob hadn't bandaged you so well, you might have died."

"I think he meant me to, anyway," murmured Rocco, and Ayoshe looked at him sharply.

"Why do you say that?" she asked.

"He waited too late to loose the arrow," said Rocco. "When the cat came for me, he just watched." It was a relief to say it, to put his worst suspicion in words.

124

"Those are heavy words," said Ayoshe, pausing in her work. "Very heavy."

"They are true words," said Rocco. "I haven't told anyone else. I told Petur it was an accident, and my fault. But the truth is that Jakob was too slow to shoot. Deliberately slow."

"But he did shoot. He did save your life."

"He took his time. And because of it, I'm like this."

Ayoshe sighed, and began washing the bowls in a large container on the earthen bench. She spread them out on a piece of soft kid leather to dry. "So you and Jakob are enemies," she said. "Why?"

"Because I've been given Torun's clothes, which he wanted, and the bow. He's angry about the irrigation system, and jealous of my place in his family. He resents me. Hates me."

"He's never had to accept a stranger before," she explained. "None of them have. They fear strangers, Rocco."

"Why?"

"Because they were hurt, badly hurt, by strangers, a long time ago."

"Is that the Bad Time Petur mentioned, once?"

"Yes."

"Can you tell me about it?"

"That is for Petur to do, or Eden. But understand how difficult it is for Jakob. Lay on him no blame."

"No blame? Ayoshe, he tried to kill me!"

"He was going to allow your death. There is a difference."

"Not when you're dead, there's not."

"Are you afraid of him, Rocco?"

"No. Not now. But I don't know how to deal with him. At home if I don't like someone, I avoid them. I can't do that here. I've got to live with Jakob. There's no space, no privacy. I can't even roll over in bed without bumping into someone."

"If that's a complaint, I take it you don't bump into Ilsabeth," she smiled.

"No. I have to sleep between Petur and Toukie. But it's not only that, Ayoshe. I'm not coping with life here."

"You seem to me to be coping very well," she murmured. "You've earned your place in the tribe. You've proved your endurance, skill, worthiness. You've designed an irrigation system that will change the life of the valley. I saw the pelt you cured the other day. It's beautiful. And I heard that you are an excellent bowman. And your work with clay equals anything our potters make."

"That's only because Dad was a potter. And I've belonged to an archery club since I was eight."

"Then how can you say you're not coping? You've moved easily into our tribe's ways."

"I do like it here," he admitted. "It's like a holiday. But I don't know that I want this for the rest of my life."

"You think it's going to be for that long?"

"I don't know."

"You feel you have no choice in this?"

"I don't. I can't go back."

"Are you in trouble with your own tribe?"

126

"No. I'd go back now, if I could. But I can't. It's to do with the way of going back, the travel."

"You came a very long way, then?"

"Further than you could imagine. Further than I dare to think."

"You're not just from beyond The Voidances, then?"

"No."

"You came by land, or sea?"

"Neither."

He glanced at her face, and saw a flicker of surprise there, a small smile almost of joy. He thought of astral travel, and wondered if she knew about it.

"I flew," he said, testing her.

Ayoshe slowly dried her hands on a soft cloth, and began putting away the bowls. Her face was serene, and inscrutable. Her composure astounded him. Did nothing shock her?

"So you are here for an indefinite time?" she asked quietly.

"Yes. But I want to go back."

She glanced at him, and saw his longing and pain. "I understand how you feel," she said. "I too have seen all that is familiar and loved disappear. What you endure is not easy. But be thankful that you came here, and went nowhere else. Here our lives are good, and free. It has been worse, in other places."

"You know of other places?"

"I have been in other places. And I am thankful for Anshur. I think that one day you, too, will be thankful."

She reached up for some herbs hanging, drying

127

from the cave roof, and cut some down. "Will you take these to Ilsabeth, for me?"

"Of course."

"And there's a coat I made for Tisha, with long sleeves."

She wrapped the herbs in a piece of soft hide, and tied them with goathair twine. "Ilsabeth is learning well, Rocco. Don't be afraid to take any advice she gives you. She will be healer, when I am gone."

"You taught the tribe pottery, too, didn't you, and how to build a kiln?" he said. "Petur told me. He said you taught them everything."

"They were young, when Petur brought them to the valley," Ayoshe said, folding Tisha's coat. "They knew nothing. They were like savages, violent, hungry, afraid. I showed them how to make the caves their homes, how to grow food and make pots, how to tend their animals, cook, and how to look after their children. The only thing they never learned was how to talk properly. Their grammar's bad."

"Oh, I do be liking it," he smiled. "I did think it was their way."

"You be liking more than the talk, in Anshur," she said, with a sparkle in her eye. "I hear you are promised with Ilsabeth."

She noticed the sudden change in his face, and he sighed heavily and sat in the cave entrance, his back to the fire. "That's why I came to see you," he said in a low voice. "I can't talk to anyone else."

She put down the coat and sat beside him, saying nothing, waiting. He was silent a long time, staring out across the windswept ledge to the howling wastes beyond.

"I've made a mistake," he said at last. "And it's too late to say anything. I didn't know the meaning of the wedding-garland, or the importance of that first dance. I know you tried to tell me. I wish I'd listened. And now I've done it, and it's too late."

"Is it so bad, Rocco? Ilsabeth is a beautiful girl, skilled in many things, and she loves you. Is it so bad for you to be promised with her? Can you not accept this time here in Anshur as something to be fully lived, with joy? I see no wrong in your being promised, even married, if that is what you want."

"I'm not sure it is what I want," he said. "I'm not ready for marriage, Ayoshe. At home my biggest responsibility is passing my exams, doing the grocery shopping, and putting out the garbage."

"You need not marry until two years have passed," she murmured. "If you are still here then, maybe you will wish to."

"I can't think that far ahead!" he cried desperately. "I can't even think of next week, or tomorrow."

"Then think of today. After all, this day is all you have."

"It isn't all I have. I have a whole other life, somewhere else. I can't forget that. And because of it, I can't commit myself to anyone here. I can't get too involved. I need to keep something of myself for my own tribe, my own people. It's important to me. If I stayed promised to Ilsabeth, it'd be like accepting a permanent place here. I'd be giving up all hope of ever going back. I can't do that, Ayoshe. Not yet."

Ayoshe put out her hand and wiped his cold cheek tenderly. "You are more precious to me than I can tell you," she murmured. "I love you well, Rocco, and your pain is my pain. But you will go home to your own tribe: that I promise you."

"How can you say that?" he choked. He got up and began pacing the cave floor. "You don't understand. I'm trapped here. I can't leave, because I don't know where to go. I don't know where I am, I don't even know when I am. I don't know what's happening at home. Maybe nothing's changed there, and time's stopped and I'm lost in a vacuum. Or maybe they all think I've left. Walked out. Gone missing. Like Uncle Alex. Just gone missing." He stopped pacing and for a long time didn't move, didn't say anything, while there flashed across his mind the memory of Alex's face. He saw the green eyes, the dark curly hair, the large Makepeace nose, the sensitive, determined mouth. The face was the image of his own. He glanced down at Ayoshe, a cold new suspicion filling him with dread.

Ayoshe waited, her wrinkled brown hands folded in her lap, her brilliant eyes closed. He came and crouched in front of her, and took her hands in his. He was trembling.

"Ayoshe, has anyone called Alex Makepeace ever been here?"

She opened her eyes then, but didn't look at him. All the color had drained from her face.

"No, Rocco," she murmured. "Alex Makepeace has never been here."

"Where, then? You know him, don't you? Don't you, Ayoshe?" He shook her hands, angrily, and she gave a sob and turned away. It was the first and only time he ever saw her discomposed. "Don't you?" he shouted. "He's been here. I remind you of him, don't I? What happened to him? Did he die? Tell me!"

But she said nothing, just sat there with her face averted, her eyes shut, sealed off, closed.

He got up and started pacing the ledge outside the cave. He wanted to smash something. He went back into the cave, and grabbed her Knowing-Stones out of their place. He strode over to her and leaned down, his shadow falling dark across her white robes. He emptied the bag, pouring the Knowing-Stones down onto her lap, where they fell across her open hands and tumbled onto the dust.

He picked one up and held it near her face. His fist shook. "You don't need these, do you?" he hissed. "You don't need stones, you don't need herbs, or messages, or dreams. You know everything. Everything! You're a witch, Ayoshe. A witch. I don't know your power, or purposes, or where you get your knowledge. But I don't want any part of any of it. Not ever."

He threw the stone in her lap, and went out.

She heard him limping down the path, and listened until long after he was gone. Slowly, lovingly, she picked up the Knowing-Stones and brushed the dust off them with her long white hair. She began to put them back in the bag, one by one. Last of all she picked up the stone with the picture of the tent. She looked at it a long time, weeping.

Then she put away her stones, washed her face and hands, and made herself a strong drink of chamomile tea.

Ten

Ilsabeth pushed aside the soaking skins, and peered out. The rain surged in torrents across the valley, veiling it in misty grey. The ground outside the caves was awash with yellow mud, and the swollen river boomed through the glimmering dusk.

"He's very late, Father," she murmured anxiously. "And he never took his bow. I'll take mine, and meet him."

"Don't be foolish," growled Petur, throwing more fuel on the fire, and making it roar. "No need to wet two lots of clothes. He'll be all right. Maybe he stays the night with Ayoshe. Don't worry."

She dropped the skins, and went back into the cave. She turned Rocco's clean clothes on the line by the fire, warming them, and stirred the bowl of stew she had saved for him. She was keeping it warm on a stone at the fire's edge.

Jakob picked up a set of reed pipes and began

to play quietly. He was a good musician, and the music he made wound through the smoke and the golden light, and filled the cave with peace. Toukie rested her head on Jakob's knee, listening, and fell asleep.

There was a scuffle outside the cave, and Ilsabeth flew to the entrance. "Rocco!" she cried. "No — stay out there!" She hurried back into the cave, and grabbed his towel. "Get undressed outside!" she called through the hides. "I don't want your wet clothes in here."

She heard him grunting and muttering, and once she thought she heard him slip over. "There's a stick in the wall, out there," she called. "Hang them up on that."

He did as she said, and stood waiting for his next instructions, feeling ridiculous. He'd never stood outside his front door before in the pouring rain, frozen and stark naked. "Now what do you want me to do?" he yelled. "A rain dance?"

Her hand appeared around the dark skins, holding his towel. He snatched it, wrapped it around himself, and went in.

Warm smoke and light enfolded him. He noticed his dry clothes warming by the fire, and the bowl of stew, and gave Ilsabeth a blue and grateful smile. He picked up his clothes and went to the back of the cave to get dressed.

"Ayoshe had some herbs for you," he said to Ilsabeth, while he pulled on his shirt. It was deliciously warm. "But I forgot them. Just as well; they'd have been ruined in the rain." He came back to the fire, rubbing his hair with the towel. "Thanks for warming my things," he said, flinging the towel across the line, and sitting near the fire. "My boots are still outside, too. And my bandages. I don't really need them, now. God, it's good to be warm."

"How is Ayoshe?" Ilsabeth asked, handing him the bowl of stew and a bone spoon. The bowl was so hot he almost dropped it, and he tucked it into a fold of his shirt while he ate.

"She's all right," he said with his mouth full. "She's made a coat for Tisha, too. I'm glad. The poor kid always looks half frozen."

"There's only her and her brother and sister in their cave," explained Ilsabeth. "Both their parents be dead. Eden keeps an eye on them, and they eat with her. But she doesn't always notice if they don't wear enough."

"Why doesn't someone adopt them? Take them into their cave?"

"They be fine," Ilsabeth replied. "No harm can come to them." She sat beside him, and poked a piece of charred wood back into the flames with her foot. "Why did you go to see Ayoshe?" she asked.

"I don't think I have to tell you that," he replied.

"Why?" She looked surprised.

"Give him peace, Ilsabeth," murmured Petur, from across the fire. He was working on his arrows, replacing the worn feather flights with new ones.

Ilsabeth fell silent, hurt and bewildered. Jakob began playing his pipes again, and for once the sound got on Rocco's nerves. After a while he said good night, and went to bed. Immediately,

Toukie crawled in beside him, whining for a story. He turned his back on her, and tried to ignore her elbows and fists. He would have given anything to be able to close a door, turn on a television, and forget.

It rained all the next day, though not so heavily. The whole tribe met in Eden's cave for the evening meal. Even though her cave was the largest, it was crowded, and Rocco found himself wedged between Cheyenne and Jakob. It was a simple meal tonight, just leftover roasted meat, salad, and something bitter and crushed, that Rocco didn't ask about. He was used to most of their food now, and he had even grown to enjoy the strong goats' meat. He finished his meal, and placed his bowl on the floor in front of him. Eden had spread furs on her cave floor to sit on, and strewn them with wild mint leaves. The air was rich with the smell of mint and smoke, and warm damp clothes.

Cheyenne offered Rocco the last of her goats' meat, and he smiled and shook his head. Jakob took it, instead.

"Narvik said you made a fine job of curing your wildcat fur," Cheyenne said to Rocco. "You must be proud of it."

"It was good of him to go back and get it for me," replied Rocco. "It would have been a waste to leave it for the birds."

"It were a big cat," she murmured. "You be lucky you still live."

Rocco glanced at Jakob, and saw his eyes deep yellow in the firelight, smoldering like a cat's. "Yes, I do be lucky," he agreed. Jakob got up, collected all their bowls, and put them outside on the cave ledge, for washing in the river in the morning.

Everyone had finished eating by now, and several of the smaller children had climbed into Eden's bed, up on a raised level at the back of the cave. Eden's cave was almost divided into rooms; there were hollow places in the walls that she had excavated to make chambers for storing weapons, food, extra furs, and pottery. Rocco noticed a large recess high up near the roof, reached only by foot and hand holds cut into the earthen wall, and asked Jakob what it was.

"We keep our ceremonial robes there," Jakob replied. "The place is forbidden, except to Eden and my father."

"What ceremonies do you wear them for?" asked Rocco.

"For the Harvest Festival, the Spring Gratitudes, and the Dance of Life."

"When's your next ceremony?"

"Not until spring."

"We be having one before that," said Cheyenne. "My new father said we be celebrating the Dance of Life, when Rocco's water pipes start working. He said we be having a feast, then."

"I wouldn't get your hopes too high," muttered Jakob, with a twisted smile. "This rain makes Rocco's water pipes a joke."

"It won't rain for always," returned Cheyenne. "You do be jealous, Jakob."

Jakob glared into the fire, and said nothing.

As if someone had given a signal, the whole tribe fell suddenly silent. Eden stood up and went to a large flat rock placed near the back of the cave, beyond the fire, where everyone could see her. She sat on the rock, which was spread with a white fur, and beckoned to Rocco. He glanced at Cheyenne questioningly.

"You go," Cheyenne nodded. "She is asking for you."

Rocco got up and stepped between the rows of people. He went around the fire to Eden, and she smiled and gestured towards the floor at her feet.

"This is a story for you," she said. He blushed, self-conscious but pleased, and sat at her feet, a little distance apart, so he could watch her face.

Eden raised her arms, and her loose white sleeves fell back, revealing the gleaming rows of metal and bone bracelets along her slender wrists. She wore a leather thong around her neck, hung with downy feathers from young eagles, and there were raven feathers plaited into her long red hair. She was beautiful, vivid and shining, like the stories she told.

She lowered her arms, but held out her right hand palm upwards, as though offering a gift. She gathered in the tribe, drawing them with her light, holding them in the palm of her hand.

"This is a story of beginnings," she said, her voice compelling and low. "This is the story of a tribe.

"Long, long ago, when men and women lived in tents woven of goathair and wool, and did buy their food with gold, and wear garments of red and green and blue, in those far days there lived a tribe. A small tribe it was, but rich, and their ways were good. They did live on shining grass beside a forest, and grew vegetables and wheat in a great garden, and all their paths were peace.

"Then one day there came a bear, and it did take away a girl of the tribe, and she was seen no more. And all the men and women of the tribe did go out and hunt this bear. Early in the morning they went, all the men and women, and did leave behind their children, safe in the tents of goathair and wool. Into the forest they went, to hunt the bear.

"All that morning, all that day, they were gone. In the evening the children did wonder where their parents were, and did worry, and be hungry. The oldest child, a boy of seven summers, stood up and said: 'We will take our bows and our arrows, and we will go and find our tribe. We will help them carry back the meat of the bear, and the skin, and the mighty claws. And we will come back, and feast, and be glad.'

"The boy took the children into the forest, and it was almost dark. And they came to their tribe, and did see a great and terrible thing. Their tribe lay on the ground, and the earth did run with their blood. The children would have gone and saved their parents, but the boy held them back, and did point with his bow, and they did see the bear, and strong men skinning it, and in their hands were spears and knives.

"And the children did hide behind the trees, and wait. In the morning the boy took them home again. But when they reached their tents, they saw the men with knives, roasting meat and sitting by their fires, and wearing their fathers' clothes. So the boy led the children away.

"Far, far he led them, far across hills and

mountains and wildernesses. Sometimes they were chased by wolves, sometimes by bears, sometimes by men. Sometimes they almost drowned, when they did cross great rivers, and sometimes the snow froze them, or the sun did burn them raw, and always hunger was their shadow.

"They saw the great spirits in the clouds, gathering black and angry above, and the spirits did beat upon the children, and almost kill them. And the children lifted up their arms and wept, and cried for the Sky Mother to save them. And the Sky Mother leaned down and covered them with her arms, and hid them in her hair, and smiled upon them like the sun. The children loved the Sky Mother, and walked in her light all their days, and were protected and loved.

"The boy led them on, on across dust and stones and emptiness where death ruled, and brought them to a place. Seventeen summers old he was when he brought them there, and he was a man and held his young son in his arms. And in this place he found, dwelling there, the daughter of the Sky Mother, a woman with long white hair and eyes filled with love. She loved the children, and healed them, and showed them how to live. And life in that place was good.

"And the name of the boy who led them there was Petur, and the Sky Mother's daughter was Ayoshe, and the place where they came, they called Anshur."

It was almost dawn when the screams started. Rocco sat bolt upright, every nerve jangling. The screams went on and on.

"Peace, Rocco," murmured Petur, rolling over. "It's Tisha, dreaming again. She does this. She dreams of her parents' funeral."

Rocco got out of bed, and dragged on his shirt.

"Eden will be going to her," said Petur. "Come back to bed."

"No one's going to her," said Rocco angrily. "She's still screaming." And he went out. It was cloudy, and there was no moon, but the rain had stopped. A cold wind blew across the cliff face, and he shivered. He crept along the wet path and across the treacherous bridge, touching the cliff wall with his right hand, feeling his way in the dark. He passed several caves, came to Tisha's, and went in.

The fire burned low, casting a dim red glow across the tumbled furs and the three children there. Tisha was curled up in a ball, screaming and sobbing, and her brother Eon was punching her.

Rocco knelt on the furs and lifted Tisha up. "It's all right, Tisha. You're safe now," he murmured. She gave a little cry and clung to him. Her face against his neck was hot and wet, and she was quivering all over. She sobbed incoherently, but several times he caught the word "burning." He sat on the furs and held her close, rocking her and murmuring.

The hides over the entrance were lifted aside, and Eden came in. She crouched beside Rocco, and looked enquiringly into his face.

"She's all right, now," he whispered. "I'll stay with her."

"She does this, sometimes," murmured Eden, stroking Tisha's long fair hair. "She dreams of her parents' funeral. They died on the same day."

"I dream too, sometimes," he said. "I know how she feels. You go back to bed, Eden. I'll stay here." As Eden was leaving, he called her back. "Eden? Thank you for telling me about your tribe tonight. You're a terrific storyteller."

She smiled, and the firelight made a shimmering red halo of her hair, and turned her amazing eyes to the color of amber. "This is your tribe too, now," she murmured. "You do be one of us, Rocco."

She left, and the cave seemed suddenly dark again. But her words had fallen like stones on Rocco's heart, and he sighed, and tried to lay Tisha down on the furs. She wailed and threw her arms around his neck, almost choking him.

"It's all right," he murmured gently. "I'm not going. I promise. I'll sleep right here between you and your brother. You come back to bed now, too, Anni. We'll sing songs to keep the bad dreams away."

Tisha's sister crept back under the furs, and Rocco made sure everyone was covered, and warm. He slithered in beside Tisha, put his arm around her, and started singing a nursery rhyme. They listened, fascinated, and Anni giggled. "What's a black sheep, Rocco?"

"A wooly kind of goat," he said.

Tisha's hand crept inside his shirt, and she drew out the chain his parents had given him. "What's this?" she asked, frowning, studying the letters of his name.

"It's something from my tribe," he said, and

despair and longing swept over him.

"We be your tribe," she said.

"No you're not."

"We do so be. Eden said." Her fingers wound around the chain. "Can I have this?"

"No."

"Why not?"

"Because it's special. I'll never part with it."

"But I want it."

"We all want things we can't have, Tisha. Now be quiet, and I'll sing you another song."

Eon sat up, leaned across, and inspected the chain. "Your tribe makes funny things," he said.

"It's not his tribe! He's in our tribe now!" howled Tisha, snatching the chain from Eon. The chain broke, and Rocco sat up, furious. Without a word he eased the chain out of Tisha's fingers, pulled it down from about his neck, and got out of bed. He walked over to the fire and examined the broken chain. He'd never fix it, not in Anshur. He swore, and placed the chain on the hearth. He didn't even have a pocket to keep it in.

"Can I have it now?" asked Tisha hopefully.

"No. Go to sleep."

"But it be broke. You don't want it."

"I know it be broke! And whose fault's that? Now go to sleep!"

"He be mad now," giggled Eon, dragging the furs up over his head. "He be mad, because we broked his tribe's thing."

"He be mad! He be mad!" chortled Anni, from under the furs.

Rocco strode over to them, pulled back the

furs, and gave each child a smart whack on the backside. There was a stunned silence. Three pairs of frightened eyes blinked up at him, brimming. He dropped the furs, went back to the fire, and sat down with his back to the children.

He heard someone get out of bed, and footsteps padded across the dirt floor. Tisha sat beside him, close, her toes across the warm hearth stones.

"I be sorry, Rocco," she whispered. "Sorry I broked your tribe's thing."

"Go back to bed."

"I be sorry."

"So am I. Go to bed."

"Be you going back to your own tribe?"

"Yes. As soon as I can."

"Be you marrying Ilsabeth first?"

"No. I'm not marrying Ilsabeth."

"Be you not loving her any more?"

"I be not lov — I can't love anyone here."

"Not me, neither?"

Silence.

"Not any of us?"

Still silence.

"Why?"

"Because you're not real to me, Tisha. None of you are."

"Your words be hard."

"I know. They're hard for me, too." His voice broke, and she glanced at his face, then quickly looked away.

"I be sorry, Rocco."

"It's not your fault, Tisha. It's not anyone's fault. I don't belong to your tribe. I never can, and I never will. I have to stay here for a while, and live with your tribe, and hunt and bathe and eat with you. But I can't love you. That's where I draw the line. And it goes for you, and Narvik, and Ilsabeth, all of you."

She was silent, crying, and he hated himself for heaping it all on her. She was only a child. He had come here to comfort her, and had stripped her world barer still.

Tisha wiped her nose on her sleeve, stood up, and went back to bed. He heard her weeping quietly, and then after a while she was silent. They all slept, their quiet breathing like a soft tide going in and out across his soul.

He was close, dangerously close, to loving them.

Rocco stopped outside Eden's cave, and checked the small bowl in the niche near the cave entrance. The bowl was upside down, signifying that the cave was closed, the occupants not to be disturbed. He sighed, and went away. The custom of the welcome-bowl, as they called it, was not lightly broken. It was the only way the members of the tribe could ensure total privacy sometimes in their homes. The upside-down bowl was their locked door, their escape from the pressures of close tribal life.

He went down to the river and found Dayv digging away at the bank, where the irrigation system began.

"The rains made a mess of our work," Dayv announced cheerfully, not stopping in his labor. "But it's not too bad. Later we be placing flat stones here, and making the wall. This will be a good thing for our tribe, Rocco."

"It'll make your life a bit easier," said Rocco. "Do you know where Petur is?"

"He's downriver, at the tanning pit."

Rocco went back along the river shore the other way, past the caves and the bathing place. He went beyond the toilet pit, and the place in the river where all the rubbish was dumped that couldn't be burned or used for compost. He came to a savage, narrow gorge enclosed by black stone cliffs, and bitterly cold. Here the river flowed swift and dangerous, and there were rapids where it rushed beyond the last bend at the base of the cliffs. There was no way anyone could get beyond that bend, unless they went through in a canoe and managed to survive the rapids. It was a shaded, gloomy place, booming with the thunder of the water. The children were forbidden to come here.

Petur was under the cliff, bent over a deep natural pool in the solid rock. Rocco went over to him and called out. Petur looked up, startled.

"I have to talk to you," Rocco said, his voice raised above the sound of the rapids.

"I be finished soon," shouted Petur, and bent over the pit again. It was filled with a brown murky solution, and several layers of skins, some still with fur, some without. Petur was turning the skins, mixing the solution, and adding salt which he scraped from a big block at the pit's edge. Rocco knew, from his curing of hides, that the salt was to preserve them. But the other things in the tanning solution mystified him.

"What else is in there?" he asked loudly.

"Bark, roots, vegetable matter, water." Petur placed stones on the skins to keep them submerged, and Rocco helped. As he leaned over the pit, the pungent smell of the solution stung his nostrils.

"How long do you leave them in this?" he asked.

"They've been in here these four full moons past," replied Petur, straightening up. "They be ready, soon."

"Then what do you do with them?"

"Wash them well in the river, then stretch and dry them, and rub in oil to soften them." Petur rubbed his beard, and stared quizzically into Rocco's face. "What does your tribe do, Rocco?"

"What do you mean?"

"Your people. How do they tan skins?"

"We don't." Rocco thought quickly. "We're weavers."

Petur shook his head, astounded, and went down to the river to wash his hands. Together he and Rocco started to walk back to the caves. As they left the rapids behind, Rocco could talk without shouting.

"I need to ask you something," he said.

Petur nodded. "Speak away."

"I hope you're not going to misunderstand this," began Rocco, hesitantly. "I don't want to break any customs, or do anything to hurt anyone's feelings, or appear ungrateful. But I want to live by myself."

"You be leaving, this soon?" asked Petur sadly.

"No. No, I want to stay. Well, I have to, don't

I? But I want to move to another cave."

"That is fine," murmured Petur. "I have been thinking along those ways myself. It is not good for you to live in our cave, when you be under promise with Ilsabeth."

Rocco grew tense, and was almost tempted to speak.

"There is room in Tisha's cave," went on Petur. "The children there be needing an adult with them, sometimes."

"If you don't mind, I'd rather be by myself," said Rocco. "Could I have that cave right next to Tisha's? That empty one?"

"It is small, Rocco."

"I don't need a lot of room. It's a good cave. There's a raised place at the back, like Eden's, where I can make my bed. There are pegs already in the wall, for my weapons, and there are good deep shelves for my clothes."

Petur smiled and placed a hand on Rocco's shoulder. "You have it all worked out," he said. "Let it be. When will you go there?"

"As soon as I've cleaned some more pelts, made some pottery for myself, and gathered up enough dried grass for my bed."

"There's no need for all that," said Petur. "Go along the caves, ask my people for their spare bowls and furs and flints. There's more than enough, and they be glad to give."

"Thanks. Thanks a million." Rocco smiled, relief and gratitude all over his face.

At the caves they parted, and Petur went to help Dayv. On his way back up the cliff path, Rocco stopped at the small empty cave, and went in. It was tiny, the ceiling low, and the firepit was crumbling in, but the cave had a good feel about it. He liked it; it was his. He would put furs on the floor for carpets, and use yellow and white clay from up the river to paint pictures on the walls. He went out, excited and jubilant, and ran on up to Petur's cave.

He was glad Ilsabeth was out. He began collecting up his things. He took out all his clothes, and placed them on a pile on the floor. He took his bow off the wall, the two spears he had made, and his quiver of arrows. He collected the plate he had made, and the spoon he had carved from bone. He got his knife and the rabbit pelt he was working on, and took his towel from the line by the fire. He picked up the bowl Ilsabeth had made him, with its tiny picture of a bird, and then heard a quiet noise behind him.

It was Ilsabeth. She had been hunting, and held her bow and two hares in her hands. She hung up her bow, and dropped the hares on the hearth. Then she noticed the pile of his belongings on the floor.

"Be you going?" she asked, her lips white.

"Only to the empty cave next to Tisha's."

"Why?"

He sighed and turned away from her. The answer had seemed so simple last night. It had been simple, when he had talked to Petur. Now, suddenly, it all seemed complicated again, and painful.

"Why?" she demanded. "Rocco, why do things be changed between us? What have I done?"

"You've done nothing," he said, stooping and gathering up his things. "I'm moving, that's all. People in my tribe do it all the time."

"You be not leaving? Not leaving the valley?"

"No. Not yet."

She suddenly swept the things out of his arms, throwing them onto the bed. The bowl she had made bounced onto the floor, breaking in two.

"I need your words!" she cried. "I need to know! What has happened between us? At the wedding-feast, when we danced, you did be good to me. So good. And now we be promised, and your heart is hard towards me. I hurt, Rocco. Always, I have loved you. I loved you when they brought you in from the river, that first time, in your strange clothes, and bleeding and crying. I washed you and put ointments on all your hurts, and I looked after you. I loved you all that time, and at the feast when you did wear the wedding-garland and you did dance with me, then I was flying in my joy. And now I be dropped like a stone, and I hurt. Why?"

He faced her then, and took her shoulders in his hands.

"I'm sorry, Ilsabeth. My heart isn't hard towards you. I give you my true words. I did not know, that wedding night, what the wheat meant, or the dance. Ayoshe tried to tell me, and I didn't listen. I'm sorry."

She dashed her arm down across his arms, knocking him away. "You be sorry, Rocco? Just sorry? You do be promised with me, in front of all the tribe. Now you break that promise in pieces, and you lie."

150

"I'm not lying. I made a mistake, that's all."

"It is a lie! We don't break promises, in this tribe. We don't lie, we don't go back on our word, we don't steal."

"Hell, I'm a liar and a thief now, am I?"

"You break your word, Rocco. You break your word, your promised word."

She picked up his things, including the broken bowl, and piled them in his arms. "Get out!" she cried. "Go to your own cave! I be not promised with a liar. *I* break our promise, *I* go back on the word, *I* no longer choose *you!*"

"Suits me! But I won't just leave your cave. I'll leave your valley, your tribe, your life." He stamped out of the cave, and the hides in the entrance swept several things from the pile in his arms. He didn't stop to pick them up.

"Take plenty of water with you!" Ilsabeth yelled after him. "There be none in The Voidances!"

He strode down to his own cave, went in, and dumped his belongings on the floor. He swore. His bowls were broken, and one of his spears was cracked. The bow was undamaged. He picked it up and hung it across two pegs in the cave wall. Then he sat down by the empty fire-pit, and buried his face in his hands. He was breathing hard, and his hands shook. He heard footsteps on the path outside, but didn't look up. The person walked straight past, down the dusty path to the ground.

After a long time Rocco got up and sorted out his things, folding his clothes and putting them in the alcoves in the walls. He went outside, and down to the garden. Jaim was there, carrying weeds to the compost heap.

"Have you seen Ilsabeth?" Rocco asked.

Jaim grinned. "It were a grand argument, Rocco. I did hear it from here."

"Where is she?"

"She's milking the goats, God help them. She's in a fine rage."

Rocco looked across the rope bridge, and up the lower mountain slopes to the herd. Ilsabeth was there, her figure small and pale against the savage hills.

"I'll go and help her," Rocco said.

Jaim chuckled. "You be risking your neck," he warned.

"If she drowns me in goats' milk, you can have my bow," said Rocco, and went off towards the bridge.

Ilsabeth looked up across the goat's snowy back, and saw Rocco. She glanced down again, ignoring him, but her fingers faltered in their rhythmic work, and her cheeks flushed. She watched the last of the milk squirt down into the pottery bowl, and then picked it up. The goat skipped away, bleating. She poured the milk carefully from the bowl into a large pitcher, which she lifted onto her hip. She started to walk to the next goat, and Rocco caught up with her and took the heavy container.

They said nothing, but he helped her milk the rest of the goats, and the peaceful work and the silence of the mountains was like a healing.

After the last goat was milked, they sat on the grass and looked across at the stately spires of the spruce forest. The singing of a few birds came to them, bright and joyous.

A small wind swept down from the mountains, and Ilsabeth pulled her fur coat higher about her neck. She wore a long woven tunic under her coat, and light leather trousers. Her fur boots covered her legs to the knees. But still she was cold, cold outside and in.

Rocco looked at her, and noticed the tawny gold of the lynx fur rich and warm against her white, wet cheek, and he felt guilty and sad.

"I'm sorry, Ilsabeth," he said. "I never meant to hurt you. My heart isn't hard. I wish it was, then all this would be easy. I don't necessarily want to break our promise, not permanently. I just want time to think, time to sort myself out. In my tribe we don't think about being promised until we're older. I need time, that's all. Just time."

"But we be not promised, now?"

"No. At this time, no."

"In the summer, we may be?"

"If I'm here in the summer, maybe."

A young goat came up to Rocco and nuzzled his hand, sniffing the milk that lingered there. He let it suck his fingers, then fondled its small bony head and soft neck.

"Will you tell the tribe, or shall I?" Ilsabeth asked.

"There's no need to tell them," he replied, watching the goat gambol off. "It's between you and me."

"It's not that simple, Rocco. A broken word is a serious thing."

"I'm not breaking my word. I'm just withdrawing it for a while. No one else needs to know."

"Then we be living a lie."

"Does that matter? We wouldn't be hurting anyone."

"Yes, it does matter. We trust each other, here. Our hearts be always open. There be no lies, no deceit."

"For God's sake, Ilsabeth! I'm only asking to keep a secret!"

She started to stand up, and he put out his hand and gently drew her back. She sat down again, but pulled her hand free from his, and stared stonily across at the caves.

He sighed, and rested his arms across his knees, and he too looked at the peaceful dwellings in the cliff.

"I'm sorry, Ilsabeth," he said. "Your tribe's different from mine. Where I come from, life's more complex. People hide things from each other all the time. They hide feelings, possessions, the amount of money they make, relationships, everything. It's nothing to hide a truth, if it avoids hurting someone."

"Don't your people trust each other?" she asked.

He started to laugh, then shook his head, his face sad. "No, they don't. And that's the difference between us. Here there's no lying, no cheating, no stealing, no violence, no crime. You live in paradise."

"We have to trust each other, to live in peace," she said. "This tribe, this valley, is all we have. Outside is nothing. We don't lie or steal, because liars and thieves have nowhere to run. Only The Voidances, and they be death."

"What happens if someone does commit a crime? Stoning?"

"That were the old way, when our parents first came to Anshur. Ayoshe forbade it. Now, bad people be exiled. What do you do with them, in your tribe?"

"We lock them away in prisons. Places of stone, where they can't get out."

Ilsabeth shuddered. "I like our ways best."

"So do I."

"You won't go back, then?"

"I never said that. I said I like your ways best."

He stood up and lifted the pitcher of milk. "This will be curdling," he said. "Come on. I'll help you distribute it to the caves."

She stood, brushed the dust from her clothes, and stooped to pick up the milking bowl. He thought again how earthy and graceful she was, and how much he enjoyed her company. She saw him watching her — saw the longing in his eyes — and the color rose in her face. He half smiled, then turned abruptly and strode off down the hill.

But she had seen too the wariness in him, and the conflict, and she followed slowly, sad, the empty bowl swinging from her hand.

Eleven

Tisha stopped outside Rocco's cave, and stood on tiptoe to see the welcome-bowl. It was upside down. Carefully she reached up and turned it over. It scraped on the gritty shelf, and Rocco heard.

"Is that you again, Tisha?" he called.

She peeped around the skins hanging over his doorway. "Can I come in?"

"You moved my bowl again, didn't you?"

"There's a spider in my cave, and I can't go in."

"Get Eon to kill it for you."

"He won't." She crept in, trying desperately to look invisible, and Rocco struggled not to smile.

"Tisha, my bowl was upside down. You know what that means. Cave closed. Door locked. Security systems activated. Get out."

She gave him a winning smile, and wound her arm around his neck. "Your bowl is not upside down now," she said. "What be you doing?"

He sighed, and gave up. "Sitting here sharpening my knife."

"What for?"

"I can think of one good reason, but I'll restrain myself. I'm going to have a shave."

"What's that?"

"It's something we do, in my tribe. I'm going to cover my face with hot soapy water, and cut off my beard."

"With your *knife*?"

"Yes."

She rushed outside, and he heard her screaming from the ledge: "Come and look! *Rocco's cutting off his face!*"

He groaned, and got up to check the water heating over the fire. By the time it was steaming, half the tribe was jostling at his cave entrance. He ignored them and spread out his towel, poured the steaming water into a bowl, and set it on the towel beside the knife and soap. Then he glared at the gathering in the entranceway. All the children were there, and most of the young people. It was the first time many of them had seen inside his cave, and they looked in wonder at the strange things painted in yellow and white clay across the walls, the clay pots containing living plants, and the furs spread across the floor. But most of them were staring at his face, their eyes wide with curiosity and disbelief.

"All right," Rocco said, striding over to the entrance and flinging the fur coverings wide open. "Come on in — make yourselves at home. I hate privacy, anyway."

They poured in, elbowing each other for room,

some of them teetering dangerously close to the fire. Rocco ushered them all into a semicircle around the shaving things, making sure the smallest children were in front. His tiny cave was crowded.

"Sorry there isn't enough seating," he said gravely. "I tried to get the town hall, but it was booked. Right — can everyone see?"

They were silent, all eyes on his face. He sat down cross-legged in front of the towel, and checked the water in the bowl. It was still hot. He took a deep breath, and placed both hands on his knees.

"You are about to witness a solemn and important ritual," he announced in impressive tones. "It is a ceremony performed by the men of my tribe, to prove their bravery. It is dangerous, especially when performed, as this ceremony is, with a lethal weapon. This." With a flourish he picked up his knife, and the audience gasped. He fought to keep a straight face.

He held the knife blade upwards, both hands around the handle, and said solemnly: "Dear God, I ask you to bless this ritual. I ask you to guide the blade, guide my hands, and guard my life. Give me wisdom, since I haven't got a mirror. And heal me, if I make a bloody mess. Thanking you in advance, yours very sincerely, Rocco. Amen."

He put down the knife and picked up the soap. His audience watched, hardly breathing. Then, in utter silence, he had his shave. He finished, dipped a corner of the towel in the bowl, and washed his face. A small pink stain remained on the towel, but that was all. He breathed a sigh of relief, then said a brief prayer of thanks. He stood up and bowed, smiling.

They broke into wild cheering and clapping. "Do it again!" shrieked Morg, almost falling into the fire in his excitement. Cheyenne hauled him back. Rocco held up his arms, and they were silent.

"Because of its extreme danger, this ritual is performed only once every three or four days," he said.

"You mean, you be doing this again?" roared Petur from the cave entrance. He had been watching from there, with Eden.

"I intend to do it regularly," said Rocco.

Petur shook his head, and his face was grave. "You be mad, Rocco."

"I be civilized," replied Rocco, with feeling. "This is a ritual of my tribe, and I'm doing it."

"Can we watch next time?" asked one of the children.

Rocco started to say no, then changed his mind. "All right," he said, and grinned. "I'll ring Eden's wind chimes when it's time for the next performance. You can come and watch, so long as you bring me a piece of fuel for my fire, or an armful of dried grass for my bed. No wet stuff."

In reverent silence they all filed out, and Rocco cleaned up his shaving things. He went down to the river to rinse his knife and bowl, and while there he noticed a large dead spider on the stones. He picked it up and took it back with him. At his cave entrance he turned the welcome-bowl upside down again, and sat the spider in front of it.

Then he went in and had a rest before dinner.

Rocco put the final portion of clay pipe in place, and packed the earth firmly around it. The pipes were not fully closed, but formed a smooth open clay drain running from the wheel in the river to the ditches in the garden.

"The joins will have to be smoothed over with animal fat," said Rocco to Petur. "And we'll have to be careful not to block them with dirt and grass. Later we can make closed pipes, if we want to."

"They be nearly ready to try," said Petur, pleased. "Jaim is finishing the ditches in the garden."

Narvik walked past on his way to the bridge, his bow in his hands.

"Going hunting?" asked Petur.

"Yes, for the celebration feast tonight," Narvik replied, with a broad smile.

"We don't know if the system works yet," said Rocco. "I wouldn't rush off too soon, and kill the fatted calf."

"I trust your work," said Narvik. "And I be killing a deer, I hope."

Petur noticed Rocco eyeing Narvik's bow. "You want to hunt too, Rocco?" he asked.

"I'd love to," said Rocco wishfully. "But there's a bit to finish here."

"We be able to finish," said Petur. "You've been working here these four days past, without a break. Go hunting."

Rocco grinned. "I'll just see Jaim about something, then I'll be ready."

"Can I help?" asked Narvik.

"You can get my bow and arrows from my cave," said Rocco, running off, "and my coat."

Narvik climbed the cliff path to Rocco's tiny cave, and went in. He looked around, impressed. The cave was different from everyone else's. Rocco had rebuilt the firepit, and widened the hearth all around with large flat river stones. He kept his cooking utensils on the hearth, tidily, in one corner, and all his spoons stood together in a pottery jar. He kept a large bowl of water on the hearth, for washing in. He had enlarged one of the alcoves in the wall, and made a rail across it with a polished thigh-bone. His clothes hung neatly across the bone, and the extra boots he had made stood underneath. All his shelves were neat. He had planted herbs and wild mountain daisies in pots, and placed them in shelves. Pelts covered the floor, and he had hung a beautiful white ermine fur on the wall. His bed was on a raised earthen platform at the back of the cave, in a separate recess in the cave wall. Beside the sleeping place he had made strange markings in the wall; notches cut neatly in rows, with written signs beside them. Narvik couldn't read, and the signs mystified him. He looked at the paintings on the walls, and was astonished. Rocco had added to them, made intricate drawings in charcoal of strange oblong shapes filled with squares, and bizarre forms on small circles. His drawings were as strange and baffling as the ones Ayoshe had done in her cave. Narvik shook his head, bewildered, picked up the things Rocco had asked for, and went out.

They didn't shoot a deer. They shot a wild goat instead, in the lower ranges across the river, on the other side of the forest. On their way back, as they passed the forest, they saw Jakob going in. He hadn't seen them. Narvik was about to call out, but Rocco stopped him.

"I have an idea," Rocco murmured. "There's something I owe Jakob."

"From your look, I'd say it's not a favor," said Narvik, with a grin.

"No. It's a fright. A good one."

Narvik hesitated, his face suddenly grave. He knew — the whole tribe knew — that the animosity between Rocco and Jakob had deepened since the wildcat hunt, but no one knew why. They all had their suspicions, but until Rocco accused Jakob openly, nothing would be done. Narvik knew now that Rocco planned his own private revenge, and the thought troubled him.

"Be careful, Rocco," he murmured. "You play with fire and thunder, there."

"I know," said Rocco. "I only want to scare him, not hurt him."

Narvik sighed, and shot Rocco a brief, uneasy smile. "I be with you then," he said.

They hurried down to the forest and Narvik slung the carcass of their goat into a forked tree, away from wolves and ants. They crept between the first trees, and Rocco lifted his hand in warning.

"He has his bow," he whispered. "He must be hunting, too."

"What else would he do in the forest?" murmured Narvik. "His girl he brings here, be now half in love with you."

Rocco didn't hear. He was creeping forward through the trees, his bow held lightly in his hands, his eyes on the figure ahead. He could see the pale buff color of Jakob's coat. Jakob moved in the forest in utter quiet, a ghostly form on the animal paths between the trees.

For a long time Rocco and Narvik followed him, and then Rocco lifted his hand. Jakob had seen a deer, a fine buck, drinking at a small stream on the edge of a clearing. He had lifted his bow, and was taking aim. Silently, Rocco and Narvik shrank into the shadows of the trees, and waited. They heard the swift flight of the arrow, and a scuffle as the deer stumbled forward a little way. Then there was a thud as it fell.

"He'll skin it here," whispered Narvik, over Rocco's shoulder. "It's too heavy to carry back. He'll skin it, and cut the best portions to eat. The rest belongs to wolves."

"I have an idea," whispered Rocco. He murmured in Narvik's ear, and a slow smile spread across Narvik's face. Then they were silent, listening to Jakob work. He skinned quickly and cleanly, and sang while he worked. They heard him spread the skin over a low branch to begin drying, and then heard him cutting into the meat.

Silently, Narvik got up and skirted the trees on the edge of the clearing. On the other side, beyond Jakob, Rocco heard a branch crack. Jakob stood up, slowly, his knife in his hands, and listened. There was another crack, further around. Jakob placed his knife on the carcass, and picked up his bow, his eyes never leaving the trees. He crept forward, an arrow placed in readiness. Rocco watched, smiling, tense.

There was another sound, far beyond the clearing, and Jakob vanished between the trees. Quickly, Rocco ran into the clearing and dragged the carcass back to his hiding place. It was heavy, and blood dripped on the soil and soft mosses. Rocco planted the knife in the ground exactly where the deer had been, the blade pointing skywards. Then he sprinkled soil and fallen spruce needles over the ground, smothering the tracks. He hid again, and waited. The clearing was empty, silent, and the blade of the knife shone in the shadowy gloom.

After a while Jakob came back, and placed his bow against a tree. He bent down, and froze. Slowly, he stood up again. He backed away from the knife, and picked up his bow. He walked all around the clearing, frowning, kicking aside bits of soil and moss with his boots. He looked around at the trees, and checked the skin still hanging there. He scratched his head.

Rocco watched, shaking with silent mirth.

Suddenly, Jakob lost his cool. He started shouting, calling for the vanished deer, cursing it. Rocco collapsed on the ground, his arms clenched across his ribs, fighting not to laugh aloud.

"I know you be there," howled Jakob, enraged, stamping around the clearing. "You be not gone! I curse you! I curse you!" And he let go a string of the most horrible oaths.

Rocco sat up and leaned against a tree, well hidden from Jakob's sight. He wiped his eyes and managed at last to control himself. He cupped his hands, and called out in a low and ghostly voice: "Jakob! Jakob, son of Petur!"

Jakob stopped shouting, and Rocco could hear him panting.

"Jakob, you do be a bad human. You do be the slayer of my son the deer, god of the forest."

There was total silence, and Rocco wished with all his heart that he could see Jakob's face.

"You do be bad!" he called again, into the deathly quiet, his voice hollow and menacing. "Kneel, son of Petur, and appease my wrath."

There was a scuffle on the forest floor, and Jakob spoke. His voice was high and quivering with terror.

"I be sorry, Holy One!" he wailed. "I be sorry!"

"And there's another thing," growled Rocco. "There is another wrong, against another of my sons. A son with two legs, noble of heart, handsome, and better with a bow than you. Speak out his name to me."

There was a long silence that time. "Rocco," choked Jakob, and he sounded as if he were strangling. "His name is Rocco . . ." His voice trailed off in terror and despair, and Rocco could stand it no longer. He burst into hoots of laughter, rolling away from the tree, convulsed with mirth.

He saw Jakob in front of him, and sat up, still guffawing, wiping his eyes on his sleeve. "This is the best laugh of my life," he gasped. "You owed it to me, Jakob."

Then he saw Jakob's face, and the arrow.

"You die for this," murmured Jakob.

"It was a joke," said Rocco, half smiling, unsure. He tried to stand up, but Jakob aimed the arrow at his face, forcing him down. His bow was drawn.

"I be not laughing," said Jakob.

"Ease back your bowstring," said Narvik quietly, from behind him. "It was a joke, brother."

Jakob lowered the bow, and noticed the carcass a little way beyond Rocco. Without a word he dragged it back to the clearing and continued cutting it up.

Narvik went over to him and stood facing him across the meat. "You do be owing Rocco an apology," he said. "You drew your bow on him."

Jakob ignored him, his knife slashing violently through the flesh. Narvik waited for the right moment, then kicked the knife out of Jakob's hand. "He is Ayoshe's chosen son," he said. "Stand up, and honor him."

Jakob stood up slowly, and began walking to where his knife lay on the ground. Narvik gripped his shoulder, and Rocco called out.

"Don't fight," he said. "You be brothers. If Jakob hates me, that's his problem." He picked up Jakob's knife, and held it out to him. "I'm sorry," Rocco said. "I let the joke go on too long. It failed, like an arrow loosed too late. I'm sorry."

Jakob took the knife, and the hardness on his dark face eased a little. "I be sorry, too," he said.

"Then there is peace between us?"

Jakob nodded, and bent to his work again. Rocco took his knife from the sheath at his waist, and helped him.

On the way out of the forest they collected Narvik's goat from its place in the tree, and walked on down the grassy slopes towards the bridge. The two brothers carried the meat, skewered on a long straight stick all ready for the fire. They saw Tisha hopping a little way in front of them, looking as if she were performing a lopsided dance. But when they caught up with her, they saw that she was limping.

"What happened?" asked Rocco, sitting down and inspecting her foot.

"I got bited," she said.

"Bitten, not bited," he said. "You be talking wrong, Tisha. What bit you?"

"Didn't see it. Imma and the others, they wouldn't wait for me. They be off to give turnips to the goats."

Rocco stood up again, and put the rolled up deerskin across his left shoulder. He took Tisha's hand, and helped her up. They walked on again, Tisha swinging on Rocco's hand, chattering.

"A bite is serious," Jakob murmured to Rocco. "Take her to Ilsabeth, when we get back."

Rocco nodded.

"Be you teaching me writing again later?" Tisha asked, pulling on him while she hopped.

"Yes, when I've done my washing," he promised.

"I remember how to write my name," she said proudly. And she drew the letters in the air, in huge and careful strokes.

Rocco smiled. "I imagine that's very good," he said. "And you get ten out of ten for effort."

They had almost reached the river now, and

Narvik and Jakob put down their heavy load, and rested. Suddenly Narvik gave a shout, and pointed across the river. Rocco looked, and saw the wheel turning. The channel stretched out, shining in the sun, and the water sparkled along it. Petur saw them, and waved his fists above his head, cheering.

Narvik grinned, and slapped Rocco's back. "Your waterwheel is good, brother," he said.

Just then Tisha gave a little cry, and fell. Rocco handed the deerskin and his bow to Jakob, and picked her up. "I'll take her to Ilsabeth," he said. He ran with her across the bridge, and on up to the caves. Ilsabeth wasn't there. He took Tisha back to his own cave, and sliced up a piece of angelica root for her to chew. Then he wrapped her in one of his furs, and carried her down to the garden. Petur was there, watching the water gurgle between the rows of vegetables. He looked up, beaming, then he saw Tisha.

"She's been bitten," said Rocco. "Where's Ilsabeth?"

"Hunting in the mountains," said Petur. "We be eating well tonight, I think."

"What shall I do with Tisha, then?"

"Take her to Ayoshe."

"Ayoshe?" Rocco looked startled. "Why can't I wait for Ilsabeth?"

"Because there's no time. This is urgent, Rocco. Go now."

"Can't Jaim take her?"

"You take me!" wailed Tisha, clinging to his neck.

Rocco glanced at Petur, then up the valley

towards Ayoshe's mountain. He began walking, quickly.

Petur called to him. "Your waterwheel and pipes do be a fine new thing for Anshur. I thank you. We celebrate tonight, and feast. Ask Ayoshe to come."

Rocco nodded, and waved. Then he lifted Tisha higher on his arm, and faced the long rocky path and the mountain. He gritted his teeth, and began the ascent.

Ayoshe placed the medicine bowl on a white rabbit fur on the floor, and sat before it. She covered the bowl with her hands, and closed her eyes. Rocco glanced at the bed and Tisha tossing there, feverish and whimpering, and fought down his impatience. He didn't dare say anything. He and Ayoshe had hardly talked since he had arrived. Ayoshe had taken Tisha and examined her, and asked Rocco a few brief questions. Then she had prepared her medicine. She prayed over it now, making ritualistic movements with her hands, and chanting. Then she covered the bowl with a soft circular piece of leather, dyed deep red, and began to pray aloud.

"Beloved Mother-Father God, take this thing I do, and make it a loving act of Thine. Take my life, and fill it with Your Own. Take this intent, and mold it to Your will. And lead Your child in the way of peace. Amen."

She removed the red leather, rolled it carefully, and placed it beside the bowl. It looked, on all that white fur, like a brilliant streak of blood. She took the bowl of medicine in both her hands, and lifted it high.

"In Your name, I do this thing," she said.

Rocco sighed, and wished she'd get on with it. Ayoshe stood up, stepped over the fur and crimson hide, and went around the fire to Tisha. As she passed Rocco she didn't look at him, but he felt naked again, and vulnerable, knowing that she knew all his anger and secret scorn.

He watched as Ayoshe gave Tisha the medicine. Then she turned her on her side to sleep, covering her tenderly with the fur. The old woman tidied away her things, and put a pot of water over the fire to boil.

Rocco stood in the cave entrance, his back to her. She knew he intended any moment to leave.

"Sit with me a while," she said peaceably. "Tell me how life has been with you, this past month."

For a few moments he didn't move. Then he came in and sat by the fire, staring into the flames, silent and aloof. She sat opposite him, and he saw, out of the corner of his eye, that she was smoking a pipe. The smell of it was earthy and pleasant, and it wreathed her head in delicate curling smoke. He was conscious of her eyes on him, black and vivid through the haze. They were like his grandmother's eyes, knowing and shrewd. Yet there was an easiness about Ayoshe, a graciousness and warmth, that melted him.

He met her eyes at last, and gave her a crooked smile. "I owe you an apology," he said.

She sucked on her pipe softly. "You do?"

"Yes. I insulted you."

Her eyebrows rose, and she looked mildly surprised. "You did?"

"I called you a witch."

She smiled then, and her whole face broke up into little lines and planes of mirth. "So you did. An accurate description, from your point of view."

"But it was wrong. I was wrong. You're psychic and wise, but not a witch. And I touched your Knowing-Stones. All of them. I'm sorry."

She puffed some more, and the smoke swirled about her like a mist. Her eyes narrowed under their hooded lids, and pierced him like arrows.

"You should be dead by now," she murmured.

He swallowed nervously. "I'm sorry."

"There is a penance to pay for that, Rocco."

He was silent, waiting, terrified.

"And this is your penance," she said gravely. "You'll make us both a cup of tea." And she bent over, shaking with laughter.

Rocco swore softly, and stood up. He looked down on her for a moment, his face scarlet. Then he grinned, pulled his sleeve down over his hand, and lifted the steaming pot off the fire. "I'll get you back," he said.

Ayoshe chuckled, and wiped her streaming eyes. Rocco made two bowls of tea, and placed one on the hearth in front of her. His hands were still shaking. He sat beside her and sipped his own drink. It was delicious and hot, and soothed his nerves.

"So your Knowing-Stones aren't powerful at all?" he asked. "Is that all just an act, to keep the tribe in line?"

"You know me better than that," she murmured, putting her pipe on the hearthstones and picking up her tea. "I believe in the power of the imagination, and the sacredness of the human spirit. I love God with everything I am. If images and stones help me to guide and encourage His children, then I use them. They are symbols — powerful, but only symbols. The real power lies in the soul's own response."

"What do you mean?"

"Suppose you came to me and told me you were afraid, vulnerable, and weak. I would tell you that you are strong, worthy, and capable of achieving all you hope. If your soul's response is negative, you remain in your weakness. But if your response is to believe that you are strong, then you release that strength within you. Your faith makes you whole. We are what we believe we are."

"So why don't you tell Tisha that she's all right? Why all the mumbo-jumbo with the medicine and red cloth?"

"Because Tisha is not able, right now, to receive my words; her soul is young and hurt, and cannot bear to hear. So medicines must do what faith cannot."

"Why the ritual, though? Was that for her, or you, or me?"

"That was between my Mother-Father God, and me. You heard the prayer. You know what I invoked."

"Filling yourself with God's life? That's pretty powerful stuff, Ayoshe, if you believe in it."

A faint smile crossed Ayoshe's face.

"I can understand the prayers," went on

Rocco. "But why the rituals? Why the red cloth, the waving hands, the ceremony? They're all just acts, meaningless, insignificant acts."

"The greatest things in the world are begun with insignificant acts," she said. "A smile begins a marriage, a loving act begets a tribe, a dream can alter history." She finished her tea and stood up, and went over to the bed. She leaned over Tisha, crooning softly to her. Then she called back to Rocco: "The child is awake, now. You can take her home."

Rocco went and gathered Tisha up, and she nestled warmly against him, her arms around his neck.

"It's my celebration feast tonight," Rocco said to Ayoshe, remembering. "Will you come? I'd be honored if you'd stay the night in my cave."

"I would like that very much." Ayoshe pulled the fur higher around Tisha's head. "Look after her well, Rocco."

"I will. Tisha's special to me," he replied, and smiled. "It was her singing that led me here, to Anshur."

He leaned across Tisha and kissed Ayoshe's cheek, then went out into the wind and began the long walk back to the valley.

Twelve

The bear loomed over the children, its head rolling grotesquely. It roared, and Morg flew into Ilsabeth's arms. She laughed nervously, and waved the bear away. "You do be scaring him, Jakob," she said.

"I'm supposed to," he growled, and turned away in search of someone else, the bearskin swinging dramatically about him. Music began to play, and Jakob danced, a slow, majestic dance, signifying the bear's grandeur and power. Gradually the music rose, became wilder and more primitive, and Jakob's dance became frenzied. He leapt and spun, whirling between shadows and firelight, savage and magnificent.

The children scrambled away from him, screaming in terror. He danced among them, slashing his claw-covered hands at their white faces. Three adults ran into the firelight, dressed in long cloaks made of eagle feathers, waving spears and yelling rage and murder. They stalked the bear, and it rushed, roaring, among the children. The whole tribe became hysterical. The valley echoed with roars and screams, and the dust flew.

Rocco glanced at Ilsabeth, beside him. She was clutching Morg, her face wild with terror, and she was screaming. He couldn't hear her, for the tumult. Never in all his life had he been in the center of so much raw human emotion, so much naked hatred and rage. Never had he witnessed such an uninhibited display of a people's fear. He tried to cut himself off, to surround himself with a protective wall of calm. Just when he thought the wall would crack, just when the clamor and screaming and savagery were about to overwhelm him, it stopped. There was utter silence.

He lifted his head out of his arms, and looked around. The whole tribe lay about him on the ground, perfectly still, the firelight flickering across their tumbled garments and their disordered hair. The bearskin lay by the fire, pierced with three spears. Jakob lay beside it on his back, panting, bathed in sweat. His long black hair was almost in the flames.

A woman began to sing. She sang a low and plaintive song, without words. It was a song of grief, a lament, at times almost a sob. Slowly it rose to a song of triumph and joy, and then the tribe joined in, singing where they lay on the ground. Still there were no words; everyone sang in their own way, of their own joy, yet together there was harmony and power, and their song was glorious.

Beside Rocco, Ilsabeth lay on her back in the dust, her hair wild across her face, her eyes closed, oblivious of everything but the song. She too sang, a high, entrancing melody that wove through all the other voices of the tribe like a golden thread in a tapestry. The sounds enfolded Rocco, transported him, and he felt for a time that in the whole world this was all there was — this tribe, this joy, this song.

Suddenly he remembered Tisha, alone in her cave. Quietly he got up and ran up the narrow cliff path to her dwelling. He placed more fuel on the fire, then knelt on the furs beside her. Her pale blue eyes glowed at him, and in the dimness her face was deathly white.

"Don't you like the singing?" she asked.

"Yes. Yes, I do. It's beautiful." He stroked her hair off her face. "But I wondered how you were. Do you want some more of your medicine?"

"Yes, please. I hurt, and my legs are cold."

He pulled another fur over her, and got the bowl of medicine off a high shelf. He sniffed it, and almost retched. He knelt and lifted her head and gave her some. She took it without a murmur. Then he tucked her down again, and put the bowl away. Outside, the singing had stopped.

"They be doing the bit where they find Anshur," Tisha said. "You be loving this bit, Rocco. It's my favorite."

He smiled, and knelt and kissed her cheek. It was as cold as stone. He wished Ayoshe was here to check on her. Ayoshe was late, and he was worried.

"Do you want to come back down with me, Tisha?" he asked.

"Not yet. When they sing again, after the feast."

He stood up, lifted the skins over the entrance, and went out.

The scene below was stunning. All the people except the musicians were gathered in two lines on either side of the fire. Each person carried a flaming torch, and the light illuminated the whole valley. At the head of the two rows, in a white robe and a headdress of scarlet and gold feathers, stood Eden. Rocco knew she symbolized Ayoshe, the daughter of the Sky Mother. Eden was singing. It was a beautiful song, spiritual, and powerful in its simplicity. She sang of joy and of love. She sang of life in the Valley of Anshur, and of peace.

As she sang, the musicians gradually joined their music to her voice; at first just Jakob's pipes, then the wind chimes and a gong, and finally the drums. The music was ancient, almost Oriental, yet there was a lilt to it, a freshness and an energy that Rocco found familiar and almost modern. The music repeated itself, over and over, each time becoming richer, more impassioned. As the music rose, Eden began to dance.

It was a slow, lovely dance that wound among the people of the tribe, touching them, binding them together. The song became a prayer, and the dance was the Dance of Life. It was the most moving and beautiful thing Rocco had ever seen. When it was over he went down the cliff pathway and stood behind the tribe, alone. Then Eden called to him.

At first he didn't hear her. He was watching a slight, glimmering figure coming around the riverbend, and realized, joyfully, that Ayoshe had arrived. Eden followed his gaze, and the tribe waited while she went and welcomed the priestess. Ayoshe was limping slightly, and her robe was smudged with dirt. She embraced Eden, then went and stood by the fire, beside Petur. Eden went back to her place in front of the tribe, and called Rocco again.

He passed the lines of people, the brilliant blazing torches, and stood in front of her. She took off the bright feather headdress and placed it on his head. He gave her an uncertain smile. "You'd better tell me what this means," he whispered.

"It is an honor, Rocco," she replied, placing her hands on his shoulders, and kissing both his cheeks. Aloud, so all could hear, she said: "This honor is Rocco's, because of the ways of water that he did give our tribe. It is his, because of his gift to us, which will bless our lives and make them easy." She looked into his face, and smiled. "We thank you. We offer you our love." And she kissed him again.

"Am I supposed to say anything?" he whispered.

"It is usual," she said.

He turned and faced the tribe. The people were all standing perfectly still, their torches in their hands. The flames glimmered in their hair, shone on knives and leather belts, cast golden shadows in the folds of their clothes, and made soft halos of their fur. They were smiling, warmed by the singing and the light, and Rocco realized suddenly how much they had come to mean to him.

"You've all given me far more than I have given you," he said. "I've given you an irrigation system, something to help your daily lives. I'm glad it happens to work, and that it brings you joy. But you've done far more for me. You've given me a place among you, a home for a while, and friendship. You've been generous in your giving, you've been patient in teaching me your ways, and you've overlooked my mistakes. You've accepted me. For that, I thank and honor you."

Everyone cheered and waved their flaming torches, and the valley echoed. Then Petur came forward.

"There's another thing to be done, before the feast," he announced. "There be words to speak." He strode down the dusty, trampled earth to the Talking-Stone, and the people followed him. Rocco took the opportunity to welcome Ayoshe.

"Are you all right?" he asked anxiously. "You're limping."

"I fell over," she whispered, with a sheepish smile. "That's why I'm late. I had to rest."

"What happened?"

"Don't look so alarmed. I'm not hurt, apart from my dignity. I forget I can't jump ravines like I did sixty years ago."

He stared at her, horrified, and she laughed

softly and pushed him towards the Talking-Stone. "Petur's waiting for you," she said.

Petur was standing on the stone, his people all gathered in front of him. Some of the children got restless and started playing a game, but Jakob made them stand still. Then Petur raised his hand, and everyone was quiet.

"Stand here before us, Rocco," Petur said, indicating the ground in front of the stone.

For a moment Rocco hesitated. He felt Ayoshe's hand rest a moment on his shoulder, then he went and stood in front of Petur.

"Almost fifty days ago, you came into our valley," Petur said, smiling. "And when you came I was afraid, not knowing what manner of person you be. But we accepted you, and said that for a time you could be our guest. And you have proved that you have come with goodwill, and have brought us joy and strength, and some ways which we knew not. We be richer for your company."

He paused, and looked over Rocco's head at his people. "I have a word," he said, his voice raised. "And my word is this: That our valley is Rocco's, our home his home, our furs and grain and animals be all his. I say he is free here, for all his life, free to marry if he chooses, free to live always among us, free to bring up his children with our children. I say he is not any more a guest. I say he is a son of Anshur, a true son."

The tribe cheered, and Petur stepped down. Rocco noticed Narvik coming from the caves, bearing something white in his arms. He came up to the stone, smiling, and Rocco saw that he was holding a white fur.

"This is for you, Rocco," said Narvik, holding out the gift. "For many winters we have been saving the pelts of the white foxes, to make something special from them. We used them now, and Ayoshe made this for you."

Rocco took the fur and unfolded it. It was a white coat, full-length, with long sleeves and a fur-lined hood. It was made of the softest fur he had ever seen, perfectly sewn, with bleached leather strips for ties, and blue fox fur around the hem. He knew it must be the most beautiful garment ever made in the valley, and the most precious.

He took off the feather headdress and handed it to Petur. He put on the coat, did up the leather ties, and pulled the soft hood over his dark hair. Not trusting himself to speak, he went to each person in the tribe and embraced them. Last of all he went to Ayoshe. He put his arms around her neck and kissed her, and she felt that his face was wet. "How can I ever thank you?" he murmured.

"Just think of me every now and again, when you wear it," she smiled.

"For longer than this coat lasts," he said, "I'll think of you."

Behind them, Petur stood on the Talking-Stone again, his torch raised high. "Now, in honor of our newest son, we feast!" he cried.

Petur helped himself to a bone from the left-over roast, and went around the fire and sat by Rocco. "All that singing makes a man hungry again," he said.

"I enjoyed your songs," said Rocco, smiling.

"I didn't know you could sing like that."

"The people do be more fond of your shaving ceremony," mumbled Petur, with his mouth full. "And your tribe's myths. You do be out-shining Eden, with your stories."

"They're not myths," said Rocco. "They're true happenings."

Petur chuckled disbelievingly, and looked at Tisha, lying wrapped in furs in Rocco's arms. Her face glimmered in the firelight, and she was panting slightly. Petur reached out and rested the back of his hand against her cheek. He frowned, and glanced at Rocco. Rocco was looking across the fire, watching Jakob play his pipes. The sounds wove through the night, tranquil and sweet.

Tisha stirred, and coughed. She murmured something, and Rocco bent his head to hear, his dark hair mingling with her blonde. He felt her slip her hand inside his shirt, as though to get closer still, and her touch on his skin was like ice.

"I do be scared," she whispered.

He kissed the top of her head. "There's nothing to be frightened of," he said gently. "Listen to Jakob's pipes. The notes from them do be like silver birds, flying on the wind."

She started to sob softly, and he held her close and rocked her. After a while she sighed, and was quiet. She relaxed against him, her head rolling on his arm. He glanced down and saw her small face pale against the fur, her eyes slightly open, still. He squeezed her, gently. "Tisha?"

She didn't move, and he glanced wildly at Petur. Petur lifted his hand and touched a place in Tisha's neck, and waited a long time. Then he took away his hand and looked at Rocco. "She is gone," he said softly.

"No she's not. She can't be. She only got an insect bite." Rocco lifted his arm to feel Tisha's pulse, and she rolled sideways, yielding and limp.

"No!" he cried, and bent over her, shaking her. Then he gathered her up and crushed her close against his heart, and wept. And the sound of his crying made the pipes quiet, and filled all of Anshur with his grief.

Narvik crossed the rope bridge, and walked up the slope to the hillside. He could see Rocco sitting on the bare rocks of the old stoning-ground, his back to the valley and the caves. Narvik sat beside him and glanced anxiously at Rocco's face. He saw the pain there, and looked away again.

"I come with a request," he said. "I come from Eon and Anni. They ask you to be her One Who Sends."

"What does that mean?" Rocco's voice was broken and hoarse.

"To be her soul-guardian, and the friend who sends her on."

"If it means taking part in her funeral, I'm not. I've had enough ceremonies and emotion."

"They do request it, Rocco. There is no adult left in their family. They chose you."

"What would I have to do?"

"Carry her to the funeral pyre, and say the last prayer, and light the fire."

"Never. Tisha was terrified of fire. I'll never burn her."

"They do request it," murmured Narvik again. He sighed, and stood up. He placed his hand on Rocco's shoulder. "The funeral is at sunset," he said, and left.

The burning-ground was on the riverbank, around the foothills of Ayoshe's mountain, past the place where the path turned up to her cave. It was a bleak, stony place, lonely and wild.

The funeral pyre, built earlier that day, was a huge altar of precious wood, piled almost as high as Rocco's chest. He stepped across the stones carefully, and stood beside the pyre. He was holding Tisha in his arms, wrapped all in black fur. He faced the river, the distant mountains, and the flaming skies. The tribe was behind him, silent, holding their burning torches in their hands. Ayoshe alone stood near him, waiting at the head of the funeral pyre. She was singing a strange, lovely chant in another language, and Rocco waited until she was finished.

He reached up and placed Tisha on the funeral pyre. The upper twigs cracked and snapped under her weight, and he moved her gently until she was lying flat. He stood on a rock and lifted the black fur back from her face. He stroked his fingertips down her cheek, and smoothed her long fair hair out over the branches and dead leaves. Again, he was surprised by the certainty that this was not Tisha at all. This limp body, this shell, was the empty vehicle that for a time had held her. That was all. The aliveness, the bright joy, the impulse that had moved her to laugh and dance, was elsewhere. Never had he believed so certainly in the existence of the human spirit.

He covered her face again, stroking the edges of the fur together. It was his finest fur, his wildcat fur. He stepped down, and lifted his eyes to the sky. He felt someone put a blazing torch in his hand, and then Eon and Anni stood on either side. He looked at the folded fur and the golden hair streaming down the dark wood. He heard weeping behind him, and the evening wind moved in his torch, tearing at the flames.

"My friend," he said, "I am come to send you on. I send you, with my love. I release you to Mother-Father God, who is the God of new beginnings, and the Life everlasting."

He was supposed to step forward now, and set the torch to the pyre. He couldn't do it. He stood there with the children on either side, the torch held in front of him, and he didn't move. The tribe, respecting what was in him, waited. After a long time Narvik came and touched Rocco's arm. "I will do this thing for you," he whispered.

Rocco shook his head. He stepped forward, and touched the torch to the funeral pyre. The flames trickled along the finer twigs, kindling them, then blazed into life in the branches. He stepped back, and watched the fire twist and dance, and the smoke rise dark against the molten sky. He watched until the flames touched her hair, then he closed his eyes.

He heard the people wailing, and the two children clung to his coat, sobbing. The fire crackled and roared, and the heat became intolerable. Someone took his arm and led him further back, and took the torch out of his hand. He was caught up in the wailing and the pain and the terrible smell of the burning, and it seemed to go on forever.

At last he became conscious of stillness, and quiet. He opened his eyes and saw that the funeral pyre was a collapsed heap of smoldering ash, and dark on the top of it was a shriveled human shape. He looked up and saw a full moon rolling through pale and tattered cloud. He looked behind him and saw that he was alone, except for Narvik.

"They be all gone home," said Narvik, coming over to him. "Come back now, brother. It is over."

"She's not properly burned," said Rocco hoarsely.

Narvik took his arm, and tried to lead him away. "Tomorrow, she will become wings, and fly," he murmured.

Rocco stared at him. "You mean — birds?"

"It is our way," said Narvik gently, pulling on his arm.

Rocco gave a howl, and wrenched himself free. He picked up a large stone and threw it on the ashes. He threw on more and more, covering the embers, the blackened form on top. He didn't notice the white ash smoldering on his boots, or that after a while Narvik helped. He wanted only to have her covered, completely covered, safe.

At last they stopped, breathing hard, their boots scorched, and their faces glistening with sweat. Rocco picked up two sticks that someone had dropped as they had built the pyre. He pulled out the leather thong tying up his shirt, and bound the sticks together in the form of a cross. He placed it firmly in the pile of stones, near where her head would be.

"This is my tribe's way," he said.

Then he turned and walked back along the rocky shore, towards the caves. But at the place where the path turned off up to Ayoshe's cave, he stopped. Then he took that path, and went on up the mountain.

Thirteen

A light rain began to fall, and Rocco was wet by the time he reached Ayoshe's cave. She was not there. He realized she had probably gone back to the caves after the funeral, to be with Eon and Anni.

Her fire was almost out. He prodded it back into life, and piled on more fuel. A pot of rabbit stew hung above the fire, and he picked up a spoon off her earthen bench, and stirred the pot, sniffing. He realized he was hungry. He hadn't eaten since the feast the night before last.

With intense weariness, he pulled off his damp clothes and hung them on pegs on the wall, spreading the folds so they would dry. Then he slipped naked into Ayoshe's bed, and fell instantly asleep.

His sleep was torn by dreams, and he tossed restlessly, sometimes crying out, sometimes sobbing. He woke suddenly, shaking and cold, and tossed aside the heavy furs. He knew that in a low alcove above her bed she kept an extra blanket, woven and coarse, and he pulled it out and wrapped it about himself. He stumbled over to the fire, picked up a bone from the cave floor, and poked the outer charred logs into the center of the fire. He got up, still clutching the blanket about him, and took a bone spoon and a bowl from the bench. He wiped the dust out of the bowl with a corner of the blanket. Holding the blanket together in his teeth, he returned to the fire and helped himself to the stew. He squatted on the floor and began to eat.

He thought he heard a sound outside, and stopped, tense, his head lifted. He put the spoon in the bowl quietly, and clutched the edges of the blanket in his right hand. He stood up, listening, staring into the darkness outside. It had stopped raining some time ago, and a strong wind was whipping up the dust, spinning it in shimmering firelit clouds across the ledge.

"Ayoshe?" he called. Slowly, he walked around the fire and stood in the cave entrance, his bowl of stew still in his hands. The sky was brilliant with stars, and an orange glow was spreading along the horizon. He pulled the blanket closer about him, shivering in the cold wind. He turned to go back into the cave, and saw the wolf.

It walked to the edge of the cave, sniffing. Rocco wondered if it knew Ayoshe, and whether she fed it. He thought maybe it was disturbed at finding a stranger in her place. It growled and took a step towards him, and he threw the bowl of stew onto the ground between them. The meat and rich sauce poured across the dirt, and the wolf lapped it up. Then it turned and trotted off into the night.

Rocco went back to the fire and sat down. He was shaking all over, and felt sick.

He was still sitting there in the morning, when Ayoshe arrived. She hurried over to him and sat near, her hand in his dark hair.

"Are you well, Rocco?"

He turned his head and looked at her. There was something desolate and terrible about him. "It happened," he said dully. "Exactly as I dreamed it. Except for the end."

"Tell me," she murmured.

So he told her of his dream, the dream he had had over and over again, when he was still with his own tribe. He told her of this cave, of the sleep, the waking, and the bowl of stew. "That's where it's different," he said. "In my dream I put down the stew, and went out onto the ledge with empty hands. And the wolf attacked me, and knocked me over the edge. That was when I always woke up, in my own bed at home. But tonight I took the bowl, and I fed the wolf. And it went away, and I'm still here. Still in Anshur."

Ayoshe got up and replaced the pot of stew with a smaller pot of fresh water. She sprinkled herbs in two bowls for tea, and sat down again.

"I know what is in your mind," she said. "It is in your mind that you changed things, and have closed the way back."

He nodded, and she felt the pain in him.

"It is not so, Rocco," she said. "Your dream was not the way to Anshur. It was a beacon, a calling, but not the way itself. And your dream was a foreknowing."

"If it was so accurate in everything else," he asked, "how come the end was changed?"

"You changed it," she said softly. "You did something. It was your insignificant act, and it saved your life. You kept the bowl in your hands when you went outside."

"If I hadn't, I'd be home now."

"If you hadn't, there would be another funeral pyre today."

He stared into the fire, and his face was white. "So I'm not going back, am I?" he said. "This is it. I've lost more than Tisha. I've lost everything."

Ayoshe said nothing, but she took his cold hand in both hers. A power came from her, steadying him, giving him courage. At last he faced what he had fought long to deny — that this place, this tribe, this time, were all he had. He no longer clung to the belief that his own far tribe was the stronger reality.

He had always believed that the letting go of the one, and the acceptance of the other, would tear him apart. Instead, he felt inexpressibly relieved, and free. It was like jumping off a cliff and discovering that, instead of falling, he could fly. He wept then, and his grief brought release and healing.

After a while he withdrew his hand, gathered the blanket about him, and got up and threw more fuel on the fire. He took his shirt and trousers off the pegs, and pulled them on. While he dressed, Ayoshe made the bowls of tea. She placed Rocco's on the floor in front of him, near the fire, then went and sat on her bed, pulling the top fur up around her shoulders. She sat with her bowl of tea in her hands, watching him through the fire. He met her gaze, and was reminded again of how much her eyes were like his grandmother's, penetrating and wise.

"You understand everything, don't you?" he said, sipping his tea. "What's happened in your life, Ayoshe?"

She waited a long time before she replied.

"I too lost everything," she said. "I too have my dreams. And in my dreams there is a Bad Time. It happened when I was two years old. After it was over, my mother and father and I went away. We wanted to go as far from the place of pain as we could. We traveled on a ship." Here she hesitated, smiling at Rocco's amazement. "Yes, Rocco, we had a few ships then. Not all people live as simply as we do here. Out past The Voidances there are towns and villages. People weave cloth and form metals into ploughs and tools and weapons. They make blankets and ropes. We trade from them if they come this far. It is said that some live in houses of stone and wood, with rooms piled on top of each other. It is said that some even print books, and have places where they teach their children to read and write. And some grind their grain in huge machines driven by the wind. I think you know of those.

"We traveled far. My mother taught me knowledge of herbs, healing, and of God. Everything I know, I owe to her. One day we were passing through a town, and a riot broke out over grain. My parents were killed. I fled, taking with me all the precious seeds my mother had saved — seeds of herbs and vegetables and trees. I was sixteen then.

"I met a group of gypsies, and traveled with them. There was a young man among them, tall and slender and fair. I married him, and we had five children. One day I broke my leg, and stayed in a small village while it healed. My husband and children traveled on with the others, seeking a place to make a home and grow food. They were going to come back later for me, when they had found a place. They went a long way. I heard of them from strangers, two years later. They had gone to The Voidances, to places unsafe, and had drunk bad water there. And they all had died.

"So I came here, to my high mountains, and I established my cave and planted my seeds, and I lived alone.

"And then one day there came into the valley a young man. He was seventeen years old, and was called Petur, and he carried his young son Narvik in his arms. There were twelve children with him. Eden was fifteen then, and all the others were younger. They came with nothing, knowing nothing but their hunger and their fear. And I taught them how to live. Those were hard days, Rocco. They were wild and joyful days, and I laughed so many times, and many times I wept. They were joy and agony to me, those children. They were savages. They fought, they hunted, they feasted, they murdered, and they loved. And they died, many of them. Of them all, only five live now. Their children have become the tribe. And now Narvik is married, and a new generation will begin. And with each new birth, the tribe becomes more a people of peace.

"My eyes have seen many changes, these past twenty years in the valley. And now I see you. And you cause me more fear than ever the children did."

She smiled at him across the fire, and he couldn't tell whether or not she was joking. He drained his cup, and got up and sat in front of her on the furs.

"I want to tell you something, too," he said. "I want to tell you where I'm from."

She nodded, and he was almost certain she already knew. He took a deep breath. "I'm from your future," he said.

The only change on her face was a slight, bewildered smile. "Are you sure, Rocco?" she asked.

"I'm sure. This place, this Valley of Anshur, is from a time far back in my history. I'm not sure how far back. Hundreds of years. That's why I can't return to my tribe, not through any conscious effort of my own." He was silent, waiting for her to speak. She said nothing.

"Haven't you an answer for me, Ayoshe?" he asked. "With all your wisdom, haven't you an answer?"

"Your vision is a narrow one," she said, after a while. "You see a single stalk of wheat, and miss the field."

"I don't understand."

She got up and moved quietly around the cave,

folding the blanket he had dropped, putting it away, and sorting through the herbs she had gathered yesterday.

"There is a dream I have," she said, while she worked. "I dream I am standing on a hill, and before me are many paths. But the paths, though vast and each containing a whole world of experience and life, appear narrowed, focused into images like slices of dreams, all running parallel to each other. And this life, this Valley of An-shur, is only one of those dreams, only one of those paths. And I have the feeling, while I am in my dream, that I stand in this place, on this path, and all the other paths exist at the same time, alongside mine, and all that separates me from them is a tiny action, a word, a human hope."

Rocco ran his hands through his hair, perplexed. He got up and went over to her, holding the bundles of herbs while she tied them with strips of hide. "I think I understand what you're saying," he said. "But what's it got to do with me? I find it hard enough accepting this place, without worrying about a hundred other possibilities in other dimensions."

"The paths are the present, and the future," she replied. "There is no single future cut into stone, predetermined, every word prewritten, unchangeable and absolute. There are choices, Rocco. There are many paths, many possible futures. We choose. We make our own future. And we make it not through our dramatic deeds, our great decisions; we make it, we choose it, through the simplest, most insignificant acts of our lives. Our future hangs on a thread, a single word, an impulse, a moment of anger, a careless gesture, or a smile. Never forget."

Rocco had the feeling that there was a vital underlying message in her words, but he was too tired and sad to think about it. He sighed heavily and went over to the cave entrance. He leaned on the wall and looked out across the wilderness, the sun bright and burning in his eyes.

"You didn't hear me properly," he said. "I'm from your future. Your future's already decided, already written, carved into concrete and steel and glass, every word and invention and act already accomplished. I know — I've lived there. You don't need to make decisions, have ceremonies for your insignificant little acts. None of it matters. Everything's decided. You don't need to do anything."

She looked up from her herbs, and her eyes pierced him. "But you do," she said.

He made an impatient sound and turned away, exasperated. "I need your help, Ayoshe!" he cried. "You're not helping. You're confusing me. I don't need riddles. I need answers."

His eyes rested on the strange symmetrical drawings scratched onto her cave wall. He saw the forms like planets and spacecraft, and remembered that Imma had called them dragons. Dragons that breathed fire and flew in the air.

"They are spacecraft!" he shouted, striding across and gripping her sleeve. He pointed to the pictures, his hand shaking. "There's my future, and yours. The travelers in the stars. You already know."

Gently she pulled her sleeve from his grip, and hung up the herbs in a line across the bench.

She handed him a large empty pottery jar.

"Go and fill this for me," she said. "The spring is just past the cave, further up."

"You do know!" he cried, staring at her with fear. "You know. So why talk of a hundred paths?"

"Just go and fill the water jar," she murmured. She was inscrutable, calm.

Witch! he thought furiously.

She looked up, and saw the rage and suffering in his face.

"I would give my life to be able to help you," she said gently. "But I can't."

"Yes you can," he said coldly. "Just tell me what you know."

"That I cannot do."

"Why not? Would the answer hurt, destroy me like it destroyed Alex Makepeace?"

"Nothing will destroy you, Rocco. You will live and endure, and go through your pain to find joy. And one day you will know the answer."

"But you won't tell me?"

"No, my love. I won't."

He stood facing her, furious and defiant, and for a few seconds he almost hated her. Then something in him yielded, and he sighed. "Fighting with you is like arguing with God," he said. "It's not worth the agony."

Ayoshe chuckled, and he gave her a brief smile and went out on the path to the spring.

When he came back, Narvik was there.

"I brought your bow," he said, handing it to Rocco, with the quiver. "I be worrying about you walking back defenceless."

"Thanks," said Rocco. "If you're going back now, I'll come with you."

"I be not staying. Imma's father is taking Eon and Anni to his cave. I said I would help him dig out a sleeping place for them, at the back."

Rocco nodded, and reached for his coat still hanging on its peg. It was damp, but he pulled it on. He turned to Ayoshe, and held out his hands. "Will you say a prayer for me, before I go?"

She took him in her arms and said a prayer for him, and blessed him. Then he picked up his bow, hung his quiver across his back, and went out with Narvik.

On the way back to the valley Rocco said he wanted to return to the burning-ground, alone. Narvik, understanding, left him and went on to the caves by himself.

Rocco stood a long time in front of Tisha's grave. The sun shone warmly on the grey stones and the rough wood of the cross. He reached inside his shirt, felt for a special pocket he had sewn there, and drew out the broken silver chain. He stood for a few minutes with it in his hands, looking at it. Then he reached down and placed it over the cross. He sat on a low rock and covered his face with his hands.

When he stood up again, the sun was setting behind the far mountains, and Tisha's grave was bathed in tawny light.

The next time he saw her burial place, it was covered in snow, and the whole valley of Anshur was radiant with white.

Fourteen

At the edge of the forest the buck hesitated, wary, and magnificent. Rocco placed his arrow, aimed, and drew the bow. Ilsabeth watched him, her breath held and her lips slightly curved, and she thought how tall and excellent he looked. He had a beard now, full and dark, and his hair was long. She saw his fingers move off the bowstring, quick and smooth, and the arrow pierced the buck's chest. The animal stumbled forward a little way, and fell.

Rocco smiled, and lowered his bow. "That's the first kill of spring," he said. He noticed Ilsabeth watching him, and put his arm around her neck. "What be you thinking, love?" he asked, as they began walking up the grassy slope towards the deer.

"I be thinking how blessed I am," she said, slipping her arm around his waist. "I have no friend who equals you. I look at you, and my heart flies like a bird in its joy. Sometimes I think it is not possible for one human being to hold this much, for this long. I fear that Mother-Father God will say, 'Enough! Ilsabeth has had her joy. It is someone else's time, now.' The ways I walk be good, so good, and I fear an end to them."

He laughed softly, and bent his head and kissed her as they walked. "Ayoshe told me something once, about joy," he said. "She said a full cup is a gift, to be received and wholly drained, with thankfulness. Forget your fear. We'll always be together."

They reached the buck, and he bent over it and removed his arrow. He cleaned it on the rich grass. "I'll come back later, with Narvik and Jakob," he said. "We'll skin it here, and divide it for eating. It's too heavy for you and me to carry back."

"It was a good shot," she said admiringly. "You do be the finest hunter in the tribe."

"You do be biased in your judgment," he said, smiling. "And wrong, as well. In the winter tournament, you shot better than I did."

He took off the quiver, and placed it on the warm grass. He placed his bow across it, and sat down.

From the edge of the trees here he could see the whole valley. The river, swollen with melted snow, surged, booming, past the caves, and on down to the bathing place and the wild rapids beyond. He glanced across at the caves, and saw that many of the skins had been pulled back from the entrances, to let in the sunshine. The day was warm, sweet, and ringing with the silent joy of spring.

Ilsabeth sat down beside him and rolled back her long loose sleeves, exposing her arms to the sun. "It is warm here," she murmured. "I be glad the winter's over."

"It was a good winter," he said. "I loved Anshur in the snow."

"You do not love it now?" she asked.

He gave her a slow, sideways smile, then put his arm around her and eased her down onto the grass. "I do be loving Anshur every moment," he said, kissing her. He moved his hand along her arm, under her sleeve, running his thumb along the warm inner flesh of her armpit, and around until his hand covered her breast.

"They do see, from the caves," she murmured, laughing, between kisses.

"They see nothing," he replied. "They be all in the garden, sowing barley and oats."

"We should go back, and help."

"Why? I be sowing wild oats all the time."

"You do be saying ridiculous things again," she said, smiling. She turned her head, and tried to push him gently away. "There is someone coming," she said, looking along the valley behind him.

"Morg," he sighed, removing his hand, and rolling off her onto the grass. "Bloody kids."

"No. Not them."

He sat up, and turned to look where she was looking. At the other end of the valley, beyond the old stoning-ground, were two horses drawing carts, and people walking alongside. They were a long way off still, coming down the stony hillside into the valley.

Rocco stood up, slung his quiver across his

back, and picked up his bow. His face was tense.

"They be traders, I think," she said, shading her eyes against the sun. "They came through the place we call Death Hole. It's a wonder their carts be still held together."

"They wouldn't have seen that other pass," he murmured, "the one Narvik and Jakob and I took, when we went out. The Senaa Pass. You can't see it from the outside, unless it's directly in front of you. They must have been traveling for many days."

They started walking along the valley towards the travelers. They walked quickly, up out of the grass and onto the dust and stones of the lower slopes. The ground ran with tiny rivulets of melted snow, and their boots were soon wet. As they drew near to the horses and people, Rocco stopped. The first horse came on, pulling a squeaking, jolting cart, and led by a bearded man in rough woven trousers and a pale blue woven shirt. He stopped a few meters away from Rocco and Ilsabeth.

"Is this the Valley of Anshur?" the man asked. His face was young, but his beard was long and grey, and he was going bald.

"You do be in Anshur," Rocco replied cooly. "What is your business here?"

"We come to trade," said the man. "We have axes and saws, and metal arrowheads."

"Those we need," said Rocco. "And clothes, if you have them. What be you wanting?"

"Medicines, and grain."

"We have no grain to spare. But we have herbs."

The man nodded. "Then we trade," he said.

"Maybe," said Rocco. "May I see in your cart?"

The man nodded again, and Rocco gave Ilsabeth his bow. While he looked in the cart, the man signaled to the people bringing the other horse, telling them to wait where they were.

Rocco saw that the cart was full of tools, wooden boxes of arrowheads, blocks of salt, and many woven clothes. Some of them were dyed soft colors made from plants. There were woven blankets in the cart too, and he thought he saw among them parts of a wooden frame. "Is that a loom?" he asked.

The man leaned beside him on the cart, smiling. "Yes, that's a loom. Do you people weave?"

"No. But I could figure out how," said Rocco. "But herbs won't buy a loom. We'll have that saw, though, and any other wood-working tools you have."

He glanced across the rough ground to the other cart. It was covered with a frame, and rough canvas type material was stretched over the top. It was completely enclosed. Rocco looked at the woman leading the horse. She wore a straight woven dress, dyed the same color as the man's shirt. She had bare feet, and looked exhausted. There were four other people with her: three men and a boy. They all looked filthy and dispirited, and an air of hopelessness hung about them. Rocco stepped back, suddenly cautious.

"Be any of you ill?" he asked.

The man shook his head. "No. We're all right.

But we may need medicines one day, and there are none left in the town."

"You come from a town?" asked Rocco. "From Tikhon?"

"We live there."

"I went there, with two friends, at the beginning of the winter," Rocco said, smiling. "We needed extra woven blankets, and flints. We had a fine time in Tikhon. How be things there?"

"Good. They're good," said the man, but there was something in the flat tone of his voice that made Rocco think he lied. He went back to Ilsabeth, and took his bow from her.

"I don't trust him," he whispered. "He's not speaking all the truth."

"What will you do about it?" she murmured. "Turn them away?"

The man called Rocco back. "If you don't want us to stay, that's fine. Just give us the medicines, and we'll go."

"You can come back with us, as far as the river," Rocco said, after a while. "You can wash there, and drink, and water your horses. But don't cross the bridge. I killed a deer, a short time ago. There is enough for us and you. I'll bring some for you tonight, and vegetables and herbs. Petur will talk trading with you."

"Thank you," said the man. "I'm grateful."

"And when you go," added Rocco, "there is an easier way through the mountains. One of us will show it to you."

The man nodded, and picked up the rope around his horse's neck.

Rocco and Ilsabeth began walking down the

hillside back to the caves. They crossed the ston-ing-ground, and Rocco put his arm around Il-sabeth's shoulder. "I do be reminded of when I first came to Anshur," he said, kicking aside an old bleached bone. "And I first talked to Tisha."

"They be having an easier entry here, than yours," she smiled, glancing back at the horses and carts rumbling slowly far behind. "They be not under attack, and they do be invited to a feast."

"They be not taken to your caves, though," said Rocco, stopping. "Nor do they be healed and loved by the headman's daughter." He drew Ilsabeth close to him, and kissed her eyes and her mouth. He lifted his head, and looked over her hair to Ayoshe's mountain, snow-topped and glorious in the afternoon sun. He looked at the wide, windy skies and the dwellings in the cliffs, and he knew that with all of his being he loved this place. He loved it more than any other home on earth; more than any other life; and he loved Ayoshe, Narvik, and Ilsabeth more than any other human beings he knew. He loved Anshur: Anshur was his home. And the joy in him was the highest and sweetest he had ever known, and amounted almost to pain.

Petur carved a generous portion off the roasted meat, and placed it in a large shallow pottery bowl. "Put plenty of vegetables in," he said to Eden. "Rocco said there be six of them, and they all be starved."

"You have the herbs?" asked Ilsabeth, looking at Rocco, and he nodded.

"Tell them I will talk trading with them in the morning," said Petur, slicing up the liver, and placing a large part of it in his own bowl. "When they be ready, they can stand on the other side of the bridge. I will cross, and talk with them. You think they be safe, Rocco?"

Rocco stood up, lifting the heavy bowl, and frowned slightly. "I'm not really sure," he said. "I'll ask them a few questions now. It's something about Tikhon, I think, that they be hiding."

"Take care," murmured Ilsabeth.

Rocco smiled. "Don't worry. I will." He turned and went over the bridge, and carried the hot food to the traders.

They had camped on a flat area between the bridge and the old stoning-ground. The horses were grazing on the new spring grass, and the people were sitting around a small fire between the two carts. The bridge was hidden from their view by the covered wagon, and at first they didn't see Rocco approach. When he came around the wagon, the man leapt to his feet, his hand on his knife.

"It's only me," said Rocco, smiling. "I have dinner for you. Roasted deer with herbs, and boiled cabbages and carrots." He placed the dish on the ground near the fire.

The man slipped his knife into its sheath, and gave Rocco a tense grin. "I apologize," he said. "I didn't hear you coming. You have the medicines?"

Rocco took out a parcel that was tucked inside his shirt, and unrolled it on the ground. It contained smaller parcels of herbs, all wrapped carefully in soft leather, and labeled with writing done in charcoal. "Can you read?" Rocco asked.

The woman nodded. She knelt in front of the herbs, and turned the parcels over in her hands.

"I've written instructions on how to prepare them," Rocco explained. "Some be for ointments, some be to drink. Ilsabeth helped. I think there's everything there you'll be likely to need."

The woman nodded and wrapped the herbs up again. There were tears in her eyes. "I thank you," she said.

"Be they running out of herbs in Tikhon?" asked Rocco, and the woman glanced quickly at her husband.

"There are no herbal healers in Tikhon," he replied calmly. "There they heal with crystals. We prefer herbs. That is why we came here."

Again, Rocco had the feeling that he lied. "I'll leave you to eat, then," he said, standing up. "When you be ready to talk trading in the morning, wait over there by the bridge. Don't cross. Our headman, Petur, will come and speak with you."

The man stood, and shook Rocco's hand. "Thank you," he said. "We can't thank you enough."

"Just give us some clothes and blankets tomorrow," grinned Rocco. "I could do with a new shirt."

He went back across to the caves and ate his own meal. Afterwards, he took a pottery jar of hot water over to the traders so they could wash comfortably. The river still had ice in it. Again, they didn't see him approach. As he neared the covered wagon he heard a sound from it, a low groan like someone in pain. Quietly, he put the pitcher of water on the ground. He pulled back the flap closing the wagon, and looked inside.

The air under the canvas was foul with the smell of human sweat and vomit. At first Rocco thought there were only old blankets in there, and was about to drop the flap in disgust, when the blankets moved and a human hand wavered towards him. It was small and thin, a child's hand.

Rocco threw back the flap, letting in the cool night air, and leaned inside. The blanket was tossed feverishly aside, and a little girl looked at him. She was deathly pale, and her hair was limp and damp. She said something, then turned away, muttering and sobbing.

Rocco stepped back, dropping the flap back in place, and noticed the trader and his family gathered behind him.

"She's ill," murmured the man. "That's why we wanted the medicines."

"Is it plague?" asked Rocco.

"We don't know for sure," said the man. "I think it's only a fever."

"What be her symptoms?" asked Rocco.

"Vomiting, headaches, dizziness," said the man. "She can't sleep, and her back and legs ache."

"Has she lumps in the armpits, and groin?"

The man hesitated, then shook his head.

"If she has, it's plague," said Rocco, and the

woman gave a low cry and turned away. "Is there anything else you people need?" asked Rocco gently. The man shook his head. "Then go, to-morrow," said Rocco. "I'll come over and show you an easier way through the mountains. We won't trade with you now, except for tools. Maybe ropes, if you have them. Give us nothing that could harbour fleas — no clothing or blan-kets. Just tell Petur in the morning that you don't have them."

He turned and went back across the bridge. He went straight past the fire, and on up to his own cave. The tribe watched him, wondering, and Ilsabeth called to him. "Be you not staying for the stories?" she asked.

He looked down on them from the cliff path, and shook his head. "No. I be going to bed early." Turning his welcome-bowl upside down, he went into his cave. He lit his fire, and hung over it a pot of water to heat. He went over to his shelf of dried herbs and took out two lots of leaves, placing them in separate piles on his hearth. He stripped off all his clothes and spread them flat on the cave floor, not on the skins. He crushed up some of the leaves and sprinkled them liberally all through his clothes, and across the furs on the floor where he had walked. He sprinkled them on his boots, and inside them, and through the furs of his bed. Everything glim-mered with the crushed silvery leaves, and the strong odor of wormwood pervaded everything.

Then he poured some of the heated water into a bowl, and washed carefully. When he was dry he took the second lot of leaves, crushed them between his hands, and rubbed them all over his body, including his hair and beard. The leaves were pungent and pepperminty, and repelled insects. He cut a piece of angelica root and chewed on it while he piled more fuel on the fire, and climbed into bed.

He didn't sleep well that night. At some time, very late, he heard someone walking on the path outside. Whoever it was went down to Eden's cave and softly played a tune on the wind chimes there. Rocco smiled, knowing it was Narvik. The chimes were resonant and low, and the sounds trembled on the night air, silver-toned and beautiful. Rocco listened, enjoying them. Then he heard Eden yell for peace, and the music stopped. Rocco laughed to himself and rolled over in the furs. He tried to sleep. The smell of the strong herbs had given him a headache, and he felt sick. It was almost dawn when he finally fell asleep.

When he came out of his cave next morning, he was late. It was already past midday, and Petur was on the other side of the river talking to the traders. Rocco hurried down to the fire, and found Ilsabeth cooking a small goat. "It is for the traders to take away," she smiled. Then she sniffed, and wrinkled her nose. "Your clothes do be full of wormwood," she said. Then she looked closely at his face. "Be you all right, Rocco?"

He was watching Petur and the traders, and didn't reply. They were giving Petur axes and saws, and wooden crates containing knives, ropes, metal arrowheads, and wooden things. When Petur came back, Rocco met him at the bridge. "Be careful, Petur," he warned. "They have a sick girl in the wagon."

"Plague?"

"I don't know. Did you touch anything?"

"Only these. I'll deal with this, Rocco. Don't tell anyone else. The traders say you be taking them back, through the Senaa Pass. Is that correct?"

"Yes. Is the trading finished? I'll go with them now."

"The trading finishes, when their goat is cooked. Be you sure in this thing, Rocco?"

Rocco nodded. "It's one way of making sure they leave. It's not a long journey. I'll be back by nightfall, dawn at the latest."

"Don't be late," murmured Petur. "We have the spring celebrations tomorrow night, and the Dance of Life. You do be the bear, remember."

"I'll be here," said Rocco, with a grin. "Nothing on earth would keep me away."

He went back to his cave and got his white coat, quiver and bow. He stood for a long time looking around his cave, rubbing his forehead with the back of his hand. Then he went outside and asked Ilsabeth how long the meat would be.

"It's cooked now," she said. "You can take it to them. Why have you your bow, your coat? Be you going? Where?"

But he was looking over her shoulder, towards the garden and the riverbend. Ayoshe was coming, striding quickly along the shining grass, on her way to the caves. Rocco pressed his coat and bow into Ilsabeth's arms, and ran to meet Ayoshe.

Just outside the garden he met her, on the

other side of his irrigation pipes, and he rushed up and threw his arms around her. "Mother! Oh, Mother, it's good to see you!" He laughed, and kissed both her cheeks.

She took his shoulders in her hands, and looked at him. "You've grown a hand's width, since I saw you last," she said, smiling. "Look at you. A man."

"Ayoshe, there be travelers here," he said, his face suddenly grave. "They have the plague, I think."

"Has anyone been close to them?" she asked.

"Only me. I've put wormwood through all my clothes and in my cave, and I've rubbed pennyroyal leaves all over my skin. Petur's not trading for blankets or clothes. Only metal and wood."

"You have done all the right things, Rocco. Don't worry. You'll be fine. The plague is carried by fleas and is caught from their bites. It isn't passed between humans, except by close contact. Did you sleep alone last night?"

"Yes."

"Then everything is fine. When do the traders go?"

"Today. Now. I'm taking them through the Senaa Pass. I haven't told the rest of the tribe about the sickness. I didn't want to worry them."

Ayoshe took his arm, and they started walking towards the caves. "I'll deal with things here," she said. "This isn't the first time this has happened, Rocco. Everything's all right. You have done all things well."

"Will you bless me before I go?"

"That will be for me an honor."

The traders were packed up and waiting, Petur had given them their roasted goat, and now they waited only for Rocco. The whole tribe was gathered in front of the caves, to see him off. Petur was laughing, boasting about his fine new tools, and Jakob was already planning a hunt with his new bow. Several of the children had new knives and clubs, and Morg had a carved wooden horse with jointed legs. Everyone had something new, and there was an air of excitement in the valley. A strong wind was beginning to blow, scattering the ashes of the fire, and scudding clouds of dust along the ground. Several people ran and dropped the skins closed across the caves, to prevent them filling with dust and grit.

Rocco said good-bye to Narvik and Jakob, and to Petur. He kissed Ilsabeth, and then he turned to Ayoshe. She was sitting on the ground waiting for him, and her Knowing-Stones were in her hands. He put down his bow and sat cross-legged in front of her.

"I only wanted a blessing, Mother," he said, smiling, "not a full ceremony."

"A blessing it is," she said solemnly, and poured her Knowing-Stones out across the ground. Dust whirled across them, and the wind lifted Ayoshe's hair and blew it in a white cloud across her face. Slowly, she turned all the stones upside down, and Rocco glanced back over his shoulder at the traders. The horses were tossing their heads and stamping, disturbed by the sudden wind. He looked at Ayoshe and saw that she was praying, moving her hands across the stones.

"Choose one," she said to Rocco.

For a moment he hesitated. This was the first time she had used her Knowing-Stones with him. He put out his hand, moving it over the dusty stones. He touched them lightly, and picked up one. He placed it in her hand without looking at it, knowing what it was. She closed her hands over the stone, and lifted her eyes to the stormy skies.

"Beloved Mother-Father God," she said, "take this thing I do, and make it a loving act of Thine. Take this intent, and mold it to Your will. And lead Your child in the way of peace. Amen."

Then she held out the stone to Rocco, and placed it in his hand. She closed his fingers over it. "It is your Knowing-Stone," she said, her eyes half closed against the gale. "It is the tent, the dwelling in the wilderness. It is you. You are the dwelling-place of our hope."

"I don't know what you mean, Mother."

"You will."

She placed both her hands on his head, and he closed his eyes. He felt all her strength, and a great peace went through him. Then she took away her hands, and gathered up her stones, and he opened his eyes and saw that she wept. She put all her stones back into the red bag, and tied it to her belt.

"You forgot this stone," he said, holding out the stone with the tent.

"It is yours to keep."

"I can't keep it. There are twelve Knowing-

Stones. There always have been. You have to keep this one as well. You can't split them up."

"It is yours. There are twelve stones, there always will be. It's just that one will be with you."

He stood up and slid the stone inside his shirt, and retied his leather belt, tightly, so the stone wouldn't fall through. Ayoshe stood with him, and he put his arms around her neck, and embraced her. "I love you well, Mother," he said. "Thank you for my blessing."

Then he went over to Ilsabeth, and embraced her. She clung to him, and when he pulled back and looked at her, he saw that her face was white, and streaked with tears. "I be afraid, Rocco," she said. "Will you come back?"

He laughed, and took her face in his hands, and kissed her. "You do be my promised wife, my love," he said. "I wouldn't leave you for the world. I'll be back sometime tonight, or by dawn tomorrow." He kissed her one last time, and bent and picked up his bow. The wind whipped across his face, stinging his eyes and tearing at his hair. His head ached again, and he felt dizzy and sick. He went across the bridge, and heard a call behind him. It was Ayoshe. He went back, and she held something out to him. It was a metal thing, intricate and shining, and vaguely familiar.

"It is your watch," she said. "I kept it for you."

He looked at it lying there in his palm, and laughed. "Mother, you do the strangest things," he said, and dropped the watch inside his shirt, with the Knowing-Stone. He kissed her cheek, and went back across the bridge. On the other side he turned, his hand still on the rope rail.

"Ayoshe?" he called.

She was still there, the wind blowing clouds of dust about her like a yellow mist. Her hair streamed out white behind her, and she lifted her hand in blessing.

He called again, suddenly afraid. "Ayoshe? How did you know it's a watch?"

She didn't answer, but dropped her hand and smiled.

Terror swept over him. He threw his bow on the stony shore behind him, and started to run back across the bridge. She shook her head, and the dust whirled about her like smoke.

"You know, don't you?" he shouted. "You know everything. You're not from my past, are you? You're from my future."

"This is not the future, Rocco," she called back. "It is a possible future."

He looked beyond her at the cliffs, and the wind tore past and the caves became shadowy and clouded with dust. "Ayoshe!" he called again, and tried to run. But the rope bridge turned to vapor in his hands, and his feet slid in clouds of shifting dust, and the wind swept him, howling, where he didn't want to go, and tore his cries to shreds.

Then for a time he knew nothing.

Fifteen

He became aware of a darkness, and of tiny bells tinkling. He thought he must have fallen and hurt himself, and someone had put him to bed in his cave, and the wind chimes were ringing. But the sound wasn't deep enough, and worried him. His furs had become hard, and there was another sound, a strange low rumbling sound. He thought of the traders' carts and wondered what they were doing so close to the caves.

Someone leaned over him. "Good afternoon, Mr. Makepeace. You've been a long time waking up."

He opened his eyes and saw Ilsabeth leaning over him. She was wearing the nurses's uniform again, and her cool fingers were about his wrist, taking his pulse. She smiled, and then looked at the watch pinned to her uniform.

He frowned, confused. It wasn't Ilsabeth. It wasn't even a girl of his tribe. He tried to sit up, and saw that he was surrounded by white walls.

There were white sheets on his bed, and there was a stainless steel trolly nearby, containing thermometers.

"No!" he howled; and the nurse tried to hold him back.

"Mr. Makepeace, you'll hurt yourself," she said. "You'll pull the I.V. out of your hand. Keep still, please."

Someone else came and gave him an injection, and he slipped back into the darkness.

When he opened his eyes again, his father was sitting beside him. Harlan Makepeace leaned forward, and smiled. "Hello, Rocco. Welcome back." Then his face crumpled, and he wept. "Son, you nearly died on us," he said.

Rocco lifted his right hand, and gingerly touched his own face. He ran his fingers along his upper lip, and down his chin. He licked his lips and tried to speak. His voice was little more than a croak.

"What did I look like, Dad?"

"When?"

"When I came back."

Harlan got up and went over to the window. He dug his hands deep into his pockets, and looked out. "What do you mean, Rocco?" he asked.

"When I came back. What did I look like?"

"The same as you do now. Awful."

"Tell me. I have to know."

Harlan came back and stood by the bed. "I suppose you're talking about your last afternoon at home," he said gently. "Well, I'll tell you. You were in a bad way that afternoon. You kept asking me what your face looked like, and you said something about a loony bin. You talked about stew, and herbs, and that wolf dream you keep having. Then I thought you went to bed for a nap. We had an appointment for seven-thirty that evening, with the doctor. When I went in at six to wake you up, you were unconscious. I still reckon you were home all the time, but the police think otherwise. When I found you, you were in a coma. Only you weren't wearing anything. You'd taken off all your clothes and left them folded on the end of your bed. There was dust in them, and little leaves. Smelled funny. Familiar, though."

"Rosemary," said Rocco. "Rosemary, to keep out insects. She must have looked after them for me."

His father shot him a strange look, and went on. "Your watch was on top of them. And that chain your mother and I gave you. It was broken. And there was a stone, too. With a tent scratched on it."

"Where is it?"

"Don't panic. It's all at home, in your room. I've washed your clothes. They were filthy. And there's another thing. You smelled . . . bad. And you've got scars all down your leg. Awful scars." Harlan sighed, and sat on the edge of the bed and put his hand on Rocco's shoulder. "I can't even begin to understand, son," he said. "But where have you been?"

Rocco turned aside, and tears poured down his face. For a long time he wept, and his father waited, saying nothing. Afterwards he handed Rocco a box of tissues.

"I've got to tell you something else, Rocco,"

he said. "You've been very ill. You've been in hospital for a week. Twice, they thought you were dead. It seems you have some kind of serious infection. Some form of bubonic plague." He gave Rocco a bleak grin. "You've got them really baffled."

The door opened, and Rocco's mother came in. She had Amber with her. Stephanie smiled slightly, and stooped and kissed Rocco's cheek. He smelled perfume, and the shampoo she used.

"Hello, Rocco," she said quietly. "You've given us a few frights this past week." He thought he heard reproach in her voice.

Amber came forward and pressed a folded piece of paper into his hand. "I did that for you at school," she said, sounding strangely grownup and reserved.

He opened the paper and looked at it. It was a crayon drawing of mountains, and was all done in brown. There was a cave under one of the mountains, and Amber leaned on the bed and pointed to it. "That's where the bear lives," she said.

Rocco suddenly pulled her to him and held her. She struggled at first, surprised, then relaxed and enjoyed the novel experience. "I thought you were going to die," she mumbled, into his pajama jacket. "I told Brent he could have your stereo."

Rocco stroked her smooth hair with his right hand, and kissed her forehead. "I didn't mean all that," he said.

Amber pulled away. "Do you like my picture?" she asked.

"I love it. The mountains be beautiful."

"Are beautiful," she corrected gravely.

Rocco's mother sat on the other side of the bed and looked a long time into her son's troubled face. She tried to smile, unsuccessfully. "We've got a lot to talk about, Rocco," she said.

He looked at the picture in his hands, and shook his head.

"Yes, we have," she said firmly. Harlan put a hand on her arm, warningly, but she ignored him. "You've no idea what you've put us through," she went on. "The police want to talk to you, when you're well enough. They want to know where you've been, who you saw. Was it something to do with drugs, Rocco? Did you meet some creep of a dealer off a filthy plane somewhere? Who else is walking around with this disease, infecting God knows how many people?"

Rocco sighed and tried to get up, but there was a tube running into the back of his left hand. There were tubes everywhere. He groaned, and lay back again.

There was a soft knock on the door, and his Aunt Simone came in. She looked stunning as usual, with her honey-blonde hair, and vivid lips. Rocco stared. It was ages since he'd seen a woman wearing makeup.

"Hello, handsome," she said, blowing him a kiss, and dropping a parcel on the foot of his bed. "I've brought some chocolates, and a few magazines. And there's a bottle of Coke there, with rum in it. Don't tell the nurses, I'll be banned from your bedside."

Stephanie muttered something furious about

antibiotics and alcohol, and went out. Harlan followed her.

Rocco grinned. "Simone, you do be a godsend," he said.

Stephanie Makepeace stood in silence for a long time, looking out the window at the hospital carpark. Then she turned and confronted her son.

"I have to tell you this Rocco," she said quietly. "I'm extremely disappointed in you. In the last six days you've seen a police officer, an expert in rare infectious diseases, and a psychiatrist. And what's been achieved? Nothing. Absolutely nothing. And why? Because you won't talk."

"They wouldn't believe me if I did," he said.

"You haven't even tried."

"There's no point."

"Why not?"

"Because they'd say I was lying."

"You don't know that. I know what happened to you must be . . . odd. The evidence is odd. Everything's odd. But there must be logical explanations, for some things." She leaned against the window ledge. Rocco noticed that her long nails were painted scarlet, the same color as her suit. For some reason, it irritated him. "There has to be a logical explanation for your scars, for example," she said calmly. "You cut yourself, and someone sewed you up. I won't even attempt to explain the time factor, the rapidity of the healing. But you could at least tell us what happened."

"Wildcat," he replied quietly.

"What?"

Rocco looked up, and stared straight into her face. "A wildcat did it. I was attacked by one, when I was hunting with Jakob. He didn't loose the arrow fast enough, and the cat got me."

Stephanie looked at him hard, and saw that his face was serious, his whole attitude calm and controlled. That disturbed her, more than the things he was saying. "Go on," she said.

"When I got back to the caves, Ayoshe sewed me up. She treated my cuts with herbs first, against infection."

"I hope she used a local anesthetic, knowing your tolerance for pain."

"No. A drug. Wormwood, I think it was. Strong stuff. Fatal, in concentrated form."

"You must have trusted her, to let her give you poisons like that."

"I'd trust Ayoshe with my life, any time."

His mother sighed. "I wish you'd stop playing games, Rocco."

"That's the first truth I've told anyone," he said slowly, "and now you know why I won't tell any more."

She came and sat on his bed, and he noticed that her hands trembled slightly. "Your father cries over you, you know," she said. "If you don't start letting people help you, he'll end up being the one to need a psychiatrist. You're not being fair to him, Rocco. You're not being fair to anyone, least of all yourself."

"Dad'll be all right," said Rocco. "He's got Simone."

"Simone." Stephanie winced. "Simone. God Almighty help us."

"She's the only one who's kept me sane," murmured Rocco.

His mother gave a piercing look. "Do you honestly think you are?" she asked quietly. "Do you know what you did, when they brought you in here? You cried like a three-year-old. You spent two days delirious, howling for that Ayoshe person. And you talked to Ilsabeth. Whoever Ilsabeth is. God knows what you did with her. And now you spend your afternoons playing cards with Simone, listening to weird music, and drinking rum. You're not here for a holiday. You're sick, Rocco. You need help. And until you accept it, you're not coming home."

He turned his face away, but not before she saw his pain. She sighed. "I'm sorry, Rocco," she said. "I'm angry. Angry, and hurt. You can come home whenever you like."

"This afternoon?"

"This afternoon, if that's what you want."

"Will I be allowed?"

"By the doctors, you mean?" She gave him a weary smile. "I think they'll pay us to take you away."

"Welcome home, son," said Harlan, flinging open the front door. "Well, don't stand there looking like that. It's home, not Death Row. Go in."

Rocco went in, slowly, and went down the passage to his room. He pushed open his door. His father had been in and tidied up. His desk was tidy, the homework and textbooks in neat piles. His clothes had been picked up off the floor, and his bed was made. His jeans and purple shirt were folded on the end of his bed, and his watch was on the top, with the broken silver chain and the Knowing-Stone.

He picked the stone up and turned it over in his hands. He sniffed it, and smelled herbs and the smoke of Anshur. He stood there for a long time holding the stone, his eyes closed. Then he opened them and, still holding the stone, he picked up his shirt and shook it out. It was clean, but there were rips in it from his fight with Imma and the children. His picked up his jeans, and turned the pockets inside out. A fine dust fell onto his bed, and he gathered it up carefully in his hands.

"Didn't wash them very well, did I?" smiled his father, coming in.

"What did you do with the rest of the dust, and the herbs?" asked Rocco.

"I vacuumed it up. Why?"

"Where's the bag?"

"Gone out with the rubbish, a week ago. I'm sorry, Rocco. It was dirt. I didn't think you'd want it."

"It doesn't matter, Dad."

"Simone's here. She's making us coffee. She said she'd stay until you're properly well."

"Mum'll be pleased. Where's Amber?"

"At school. She'll be home, soon."

"I suppose I'll have to go back to school, again."

"There's not much point, until next year. You missed sitting your exams."

"How's Tallulah?"

"Don't you remember?"

"Remember what?"

"She visited you in the hospital."

"Did I talk to her?"

"You must have said something. She seemed upset when she left."

Rocco sighed, and sat down on the edge of the bed. He opened his hand and looked at the stone.

Simone poked her head around the bedroom door. "Coffee's ready," she said. "I see you've found your stone, Rocco. Your father was going to throw it out. I threatened to smash all his gnomes if he did."

For the first time in a week, Rocco smiled. "Thanks," he said. "I'll drill a hole in it, and hang it around my neck."

"I've already made something," said Simone. "I hope you like it." She handed him a small drawstring bag, exactly the right size to hold the stone. The bag was made of fine soft leather, handsewn, and the string was a leather thong long enough to go over his head. The bag and the thong were dyed a rich earthy red.

Rocco looked up at Simone, joyful and astounded. "How did you know?" he asked.

"Know what?"

"Doesn't matter." Rocco put the stone in the bag, and slipped it over his head. He put the bag inside his shirt, next to his skin. For the first time since leaving Anshur, he felt at peace. He put his arm around Simone's neck, and kissed her cheek. "Thanks," he said, smiling. "Now, where's that coffee? I haven't had a cup of coffee for months."

* * *

Rocco started to walk into the lounge, but realized Simone was busy. She was sitting on the sofa with her back to him, talking into a tape recorder. Her voice was low, and she laughed sometimes, softly. Rocco knocked on the edge of the door. Simone switched off the recorder, and turned around.

"Come in, Rocco. You don't have to knock. It's your home."

"Are you busy?"

"Making a tape to a gorgeous man, that's all."

"I was wondering if you'd like to come for a walk."

"I'd love to. Where do you want to go?"

He shrugged. "Anywhere. Anywhere there's grass, and dust, and wind."

"There's not going to be much dust and wind," she said. "It's going to rain. Wait a minute, will you?"

She was back in a few moments, her lips freshly reddened, and her umbrella in her hands.

"I know where we can go," she said, as they stepped outside. "That lovely park in Montague Street. I used to take you there, in your pram."

He laughed, and she watched him sideways, smiling.

"You used to put me on that long slide," he said. "The dinosaur's neck. I was terrified. You came on it with me once, and we got stuck. Remember? And that old man told you off."

"I remember. You hated slides. You always played in the gardens, and hid in that little cave behind the fountain. You hid there for three hours once. We had the police and everyone looking for you. Are you all right?"

"I be fine," he said, but his face was grief-stricken again.

Simone sighed. "You do not be fine," she said. "You be suffering inside."

He looked at her intently. Then his face softened, and he almost smiled. "That sounds so good," he murmured.

"What? Your suffering?"

"Your words. They do be good for me, so good. Oh, Simone. Sometimes I think I'll go mad if I can't go back. Have you ever wanted anything so much, you think if you can't have it something inside you will break, and die of longing and pain? Sometimes I think I'd rather be dead, than live outside Anshur. I miss it, Simone. I miss the mountains, the caves, the wind chimes, the hunting, the fires, the bathing-times, the evenings, the nights. I miss Ayoshe. I miss Narvik, and Ilsabeth. God, I miss Ilsabeth. She was my promised wife."

He stopped talking and walked on, breathing hard. Simone said nothing. They came to the park, and sat on a wooden seat under a pine tree. Rocco wiped the back of his hand across his face. He stared across the grass, but his eyes saw a valley with a river running through.

"I lived in a cave," he said. "For an autumn, a winter, and the beginning of a spring, I lived in the cave dwellings of Anshur."

He told everything, then. Everything, from the first words with Tisha on the stoning-ground, to his last memory of Ayoshe, pale and cloudy with dust, across the bridge.

When he finished, it was evening, and the park was grey and glimmering under a veil of rain. Streetlights winked along the far side, and beyond them car lights moved slowly through the dusk.

Rocco and Simone were both soaking wet. Her umbrella was still rolled up on the seat between them. She gave him a pensive smile, and took his hand.

"I think you must tell a story better than Eden did," she said. "Now you have me crying for Anshur, too. It must be an amazing place."

Rocco nodded. He looked older, and tired, but the terrible desperation had gone. Rain dripped off his hair and trickled down his face. He looked at Simone, and grinned.

"You look terrific when you're wet," he said.

She smiled, and stood up. "That's what Michael says," she said. "We bathe together, with wine and candlelight."

"Is he that gorgeous man you're doing the tape for?" he asked, as they began walking back.

"He certainly is. He's a musician. Travels a lot, gives performances all over the world. He owns a retreat away up in the mountains. We go there whenever he's home — go fishing, tramping, even hunting sometimes, if we feel like venison for dinner. It's like paradise there."

Rocco grinned. "You two would love Anshur," he said.

The smile died on Simone's face, and her eyes became troubled and grave. She stopped under a streetlight and gave Rocco a long, questioning look. "Rocco, Ayoshe said Anshur was a possible future, didn't she?"

"Yes. But so what?"

"Doesn't that worry you?"

"Why should it? Anshur's thousands of years away, after another ice age, or a collision with a meteorite, or something."

"What if it's not that far ahead?" she asked, and her lips were pale in the harsh blue light. "What if it's only a few years ahead?"

"It couldn't be, Simone. The whole climate, the land, everything, was different. There were hardly any birds. There were more insects than there are now. The only trees were in that little forest Ayoshe planted. The climate was cold. Even spring wasn't really warm. It wasn't anything like what we have now. It's after some huge event that kills off everything we have, changes the whole world we know. Like another ice age, or the earth tilting off its axis."

"Or a nuclear war," she said.

For a few moments he was stunned. Then he gave a hard laugh and started walking again. Simone hurried after him, her heels clicking loudly on the shining pavement. Other people walked past on their way home from work, their raincoats gleaming in the streetlight.

"It is possible," she said, drawing alongside him. He refused to look at her, and stared straight ahead, his face like a mask. "Why else would she give you the Knowing-Stone?" Simone asked. "Why else would she call you the dwelling-place of hope? Surely she thought you could change things, could do something to stop it."

"To stop a nuclear war?" he asked. "Me?

Rocco Makepeace? Plague victim, and dreamer supreme? Me? Rocco, who's just spent two weeks with a psychiatrist, trying to unscrew my head? Come off it, Simone!"

"You didn't imagine it all, Rocco. You've got your wildcat scars to prove it, and that stone around your neck."

"It's beginning to feel like a millstone."

"Maybe it's meant to."

He stopped walking, and gripped her sleeve. "Listen, Simone. I don't want to discuss this any more. In a moment of weakness, I told you about Anshur. Now forget it. Don't ask me anything, don't discuss it. I don't want to talk to you about it ever again." He walked off, and turned down his own driveway.

Simone sighed heavily, and glanced up at the evening skies. It had stopped raining now, and a crescent moon sailed through the ragged clouds.

For the first time in her life, she prayed.

Through all the difficult months ahead, Anshur haunted Simone as it haunted Rocco. It was a light and a shadow, a joy and a pain, a beautiful ideal and a most terrible foreboding.

She thought of Rocco wrestling with the darkness, loving Anshur with everything in him, yet fighting to revoke it, to wipe it out totally. She saw him come home white with exhaustion after his peace meetings, watched him frantically write letters to people all over the world, and heard him weep with frustration and anger over the replies.

Finally, unable to help him, she went home. Gradually his letters to her became less agonized, and he spoke of his schoolwork, and threw himself into studying.

He thought of Ayoshe more than of Anshur, and the memory of her was in his life like a light, and gave him peace at last.

Sixteen

Simone stopped outside Rocco's door and knocked. "Come in," he called, and she went in. He was standing over by the window, still wearing his black suit, and he was holding a model plane in his hands.

"She always asked me about these," he said, putting it down. "I never dared throw them out. Uncle Alex gave them to me, before he disappeared."

"You visited your grandmother often, didn't you?" Simone murmured, sitting on the edge of his desk. "You were close. She thought a lot of you."

"She reminded me of Ayoshe," he said.

Simone looked up at the paintings on the opposite wall, above his bed. There was a large painting he had done of Anshur, with the valley white with snow, and the dwellings in the cliff looking secret and homely behind their dark skins. Beside the painting was a pencil sketch of a noble old woman with intense black eyes and long white hair.

"Do you still think about Ayoshe?" Simone asked. "It's three years since that awful time."

He laughed, and sat on the bed opposite her. "It wasn't awful," he said.

"Those first six months were, after you came back. I was afraid for you, Rocco. We all were. We thought you were cracking up."

"You weren't so calm yourself," he said, remembering. "You were so scared, you wouldn't even listen to the news."

"Well nothing's happened, has it?" she said. "You finished your exams, passed with honors, and now you're training as a teacher. You like it?"

"I love it. And what about you, Simone? I heard you making a tape before. To the same gorgeous man, with the water and the wine and the candlelight?"

"The same one."

"Why don't you get married?"

"Because things are great, just the way they are. Besides, he travels a lot. He leaves on another world tour next week. He's hardly ever home, Rocco. If I were his wife, I'd resent his going away all the time. As it is, I just enjoy his homecomings."

A sadness passed across Rocco's face.

"You still think of Ilsabeth?" Simone asked gently.

"I think of her every day. And Ayoshe, and Narvik, and the others. I wonder what happened to them, to Anshur, when I left. I wonder whether they still live in that valley, in another dimension somewhere, or whether we've already crossed to another future path, and they live somewhere else. Maybe they haven't even been born. Maybe Anshur is a valley somewhere in northern Europe, with a river without fishing traps running past a cliff with empty caves."

"You are happy now, aren't you?" Simone asked. "You're not still wishing you were back in Anshur?"

He smiled. "No. They're good memories, Simone. Ayoshe said once that a full cup is a gift, to be received and wholly drained, with thankfulness. I received Anshur, and I drained the cup, every drop. If it is the only full cup I ever have, life will be worth it."

"Have you met anyone else special?"

He smiled again, and nodded. "Yes. There's a girl back at training college. Her name's Erika."

"Long black hair and blue eyes?"

"Short blonde hair, and grey eyes. And terrific legs."

Simone laughed. Amber came running in, excited and breathless.

"They've brought her box from the hospital!" she cried. "All Gran's things. Are you going to come and look?"

Rocco stood up. "We've just been to a funeral, not a Christmas party," he said, winding her long plait around his hand, and pulling her close. "There'll be nothing exciting in the box. Just talcum powder and photos, and maybe some of her clothes."

"There might be," she said, swinging with her

arms around his waist. She was twelve now, with long hair the same deep black as his. "There might be a surprise."

"Go and look then," he said, and she raced off to the kitchen. "Mercenary little toad," muttered Rocco, but Simone shook her head.

"She didn't even know your grandmother," she said. "She only knew a confused old woman in a pink bed jacket."

"She wasn't all that confused," murmured Rocco. "Not all the time."

He and Simone followed Amber out to the kitchen. His parents were already there, sitting down, and the box was on the table in front of them.

"It's only a shoe box," grumbled Amber, disappointed.

"What did you expect?" murmured her mother. "A treasure chest?"

Rocco leaned against the bench, feeling suddenly apprehensive. He put his hand to his chest, where the Knowing-Stone was, and felt its smooth, comfortable form through his shirt.

Harlan took the lid off the box, and Amber leaned eagerly over it. "It's nothing!" she wailed. "Just old letters, and things." She started pulling things out of the box, and Stephanie slapped her hand away.

"They're her letters," Harlan said, picking several up. "The ones she wrote to Russia. The nurses must have saved them." He sorted through them, frowning. "Hold on," he said, singling one out. "Here's one addressed to her. It's from — from Baikonur, in Russia. That's where they launch all their spaceships, isn't it?"

Rocco leaned forward, his face flushed and intense. For some strange reason he could think only of the drawings on Ayoshe's cave wall, the weird symmetrical diagrams of planets and spacecraft.

Slowly, Harlan removed the letter from the envelope. He unfolded it and spread it out on the table, and looked at the name on the bottom of the page. He glanced at the other letters scattered across the table, all written in his mother's small, neat style. They were all addressed to Alexei Bibikov. Then he looked again at the letter unfolded before him, and covered his face with his hand.

"What is it?" Stephanie asked impatiently. She picked the letter up and read the name at the bottom. "It's from Alexei Bibikov," she said. "That's the woman your mother wrote to. She really did exist."

"It's not a she," said Harlan, taking the letter from her. "It's a he. Alexei. Alex. It's my brother, Alex." He got up and went over to the bench by Rocco. He leaned over it, and was so white, Rocco thought he was going to be ill. "It all falls into place now," said Harlan, in a low voice. "He defected to Russia. And only Mum knew, and no one posted her letters."

"I did," said Rocco, and everyone looked at him. "I posted one once, to Alexei Bibikov."

"Thank God someone did," murmured Simone.

Harlan sighed, and turned around. He gave the letter to Rocco. "You read it, son."

Rocco took the letter, wishing his hands were steadier. The writing was beautiful and strong, and done with a fountain pen. Parts of it were smudged, as if someone had wept over it.

"It's dated April sixteenth, this year," he said. "Six months ago."

"Well, read it," said Stephanie.

Rocco began. *"Dearest Mother, I cannot tell you what your letter meant to me. It's a miracle it arrived. It was so crumpled, and covered with orange stains . . . with orange stains of some sort . . ."*

"Do you want me to read it?" asked Simone.

"No. No, I'll read it," said Rocco. "The orange stains were tomato sauce. I threw the letter in a rubbish bin, outside a takeaway place. I nearly didn't post it."

"Carry on," said his father gently.

". . . and covered with orange stains of some sort, and the address was smudged. But it arrived, and my life hasn't been the same since. You had mentioned an old pen friend you wanted me to visit. So I did, and I became very close to her and her family. I suppose they replaced my own family in many ways. I spent a lot of time with them. Especially, I spent time with Shura. She's four years younger than me, and a doctor. She's interested in herbal healing and alternative methods of treating disease.

"Two years ago Shura and I were married. I wrote and told you, but never heard back. Maybe you never got my letter, or the wedding photos. It grieves me constantly that our lives are so far apart, that our letters so often go

astray. Maybe you've never written, except for that one time. Why only once? Is it so hard to forgive, to accept that I'm here, that I've made another life for myself? My work here as a cosmonaut means everything to me. Russia is my home now. I wish you could accept that.

"My only regret is that I've lost ties with my family. I miss Simone and Harlan, and Harlan's children. Couldn't you find it in your heart to forget your anger with me, your shame, or whatever it is you feel, and tell them where I am? I've been thinking a lot about them lately. I suppose Rocco's a young man now, and looking more like me than ever. I always felt close to Rocco, and not just because of our physical likeness. Please give him my best regards. Maybe he'd like to write. That would mean a great deal to me.

"And now to my main, marvelous news.

"Shura and I have a child. More than ever now I wish you could come to visit us. I wish all our family differences, all our hurts, could be healed. Maybe they will be. Maybe somehow, through my daughter, there will be reconciliation and peace. I hope so.

"She was born a month ago, and already our family resemblance is strong in her. She has a knowing face, for one so young; thick brown hair, a Makepeace nose (slightly modified!) and your black eyes. We have called her Ayoshe..."

The letter dropped from Rocco's hands, and for a few moments he didn't move. Then he left the room.

Harlan bent down and picked up the letter.

"It can't be," said Stephanie firmly. "He read the name incorrectly. "What does it say Harlan?"

Harlan looked at the letter, and wiped his hand across his eyes. "It is Ayoshe," he said.

Simone stood up and went to find Rocco. He was standing in his room, looking at the pictures he had done of Anshur and Ayoshe. The small red leather bag was on the bed, the Knowing-Stone in his hands.

Simone sat down and looked at him. "What are you going to do?" she asked, distraught.

"Do? Nothing. I'm not doing anything."

"But you have to! You told me Ayoshe was two years old when the Bad Time started. Rocco we've got eighteen months!"

Rocco's face was tranquil, his mouth slightly smiling. "Ayoshe also told me that the greatest things in the world are not the results of great decisions or dramatic deeds. She said our greatest achievements are begun with the most insignificant acts. Our future hangs on a thread. Hers certainly did."

He put the Knowing-Stone back in the bag, and hung it around his neck. "I'm not doing anything," he said again calmly. "If what has to be done is so small, so insignificant, I've probably already done it."

"You'd know if you wiped out Anshur," she said softly. "Everything in you would know."

He gave her a slow, enigmatic smile. "Would I?" he said. "Maybe I won't be the one to do it, Simone. Maybe I'm only the catalyst, the beginning in a whole series of events. Maybe it's not just one single thing I do; maybe it's something huge that we're all involved in — me, you, Grandma, Alex. Maybe our whole family's involved, maybe we all play a part. I might be only a link in the chain."

"We'd know," she said uneasily, "if we were doing something significant."

"Would we?" he asked gently. "Did I know, when I posted Grandma's letter, that it would bring Ayoshe into the world? We don't know, Simone. We don't know anything. We're voices in the wind. We all say our piece, play our part, and move on. And we never know the difference we've made."

"I still think you'd know if you canceled Anshur," she murmured. "It's part of you, Rocco. It's part of all of us, now. Especially Alex."

Rocco sat beside her, his dark head bent, his hands clenched on his thighs. Simone looked sideways into his face, then took one of his hands and held it in both her own. It was something Ayoshe had done long ago, and the action had given him encouragement and peace. It gave him the same now. For a long time neither of them spoke. Then, quietly, Simone let go his hand, and stood up. "I'll be out in the garden if you need me," she said, and left.

Rocco remained sitting there, his fingers wrapped around the Knowing-Stone, his eyes on the opposite wall, seeing nothing. He was thinking of Alex.

Alex, who had vanished from their lives without a trace; whose only link with them had been a helpless, deranged old woman in a hospital, who muttered about Russia and Mars and her missing son — and to whom they never listened. And Alex, the misfit, the black sheep of the family, had remained cut off, alienated, apart. He thought of Alex's wife, who loved herbs and alternative medicines, and God. And he thought, with panic and love, of their child. Their child, with her mother's wisdom, and her grandmother's black and knowing eyes. Their child, his cousin. Ayoshe, newborn.

He thought of that first time they met, out there in the dust beside the Talking-Stone; and he remembered how, in that first fleeting moment, she had known who he was. He remembered those quiet, unguarded times when he had caught her looking at him, and seen the recognition and sorrow in her eyes. He thought of the times he had felt she knew him, recognized him, loved him. "You are more precious to me than I can tell you," she had said. Because you are my family, my kinsman, my blood. Because in you I see my father. And he had almost seen it, then — but she had veiled the truth, closed it off again. He remembered his anger with her, his helpless rage, his almost hate. And her love. Always, her love.

He got up and went over to his bedroom window. He flung it open wide, and leaned out and looked across the sun-drenched garden. The wind rustled the curtain, and breathed across his face. For the first time in many months he felt the old pain, the longing. In that moment he would have given all he had to smell the smoke of Anshur, and to hear Tisha's voice again, calling him, singing in the wind.

But the moment, the longing passed; and he closed the window, shutting out the wind, and sat at his old desk. He opened the top drawer, sorted through the contents, and took out some paper and a pen. For over an hour he wrote.

Simone gave up strangling the large weed and stood up and watched as Rocco came towards her across the lawn. He had changed into jeans and a sweatshirt, and was looking relaxed and peaceful again.

"Harlan's great on goblins, but not so hot on gardening," Simone said, smiling. "I decided to wage war on the weeds."

"You don't have to," said Rocco. "When the jungle starts climbing in the windows, Dad gets a gardener in."

"It's healing having my hands in the soil," she said. "I don't mind." She glanced at the thick blue envelope in his hands. "Been writing to your long-legged lady?"

Rocco smiled, but shook his head. "No. Not to her. But I want to post it now. Do you feel like a walk?"

"Yes, I do. But give me a minute to clean up."

Rocco sat on the front steps and waited for her, the letter in his hands. A sudden breeze sprang up, swirling dust and leaves across his feet. He noticed one of his father's gnomes peering out from under a dandelion, grinning. He grinned back, and pulled a face at it. Simone came out, hands washed, sleek hair brushed, and fresh lipstick on. She slammed the door behind her, and they walked out into the street.

"I read the rest of Alex's letter," Simone said

hesitantly, when they'd been walking for a while. "He mentioned a bit about his life. It seems he's been quite successful in Russia. He and Shura have very influential friends. Scientists, engineers, people like that."

"I suppose he's important himself," said Rocco. "He and his family would be protected, if there was a disaster. There'd be special underground shelters for the country's top people. And Ayoshe and her mother and father survived . . . would survive, I mean. They'd be among the few who would."

"I wasn't thinking about that side of it," murmured Simone. "I was thinking about all those letters you wrote, when you first came back from Anshur — all those frantic letters to overseas leaders, to people with power to prevent a war."

"It was pointless, anyway," said Rocco. "Nobody listened."

"I know. Because you were barking up the wrong tree. The real answer lies closer to home."

Rocco stopped and stared at her.

"Rocco — you said before that we all play a part in this, that you and I, Grandma and Alex, we all say our piece and play our part, and move on. Well, I think Alex doesn't just play a part. I think he's the whole answer." She stopped, panting slightly, her grey eyes vivid and intense. "He's been there all the time, Rocco, right in the middle, and we didn't see it."

Rocco took a deep breath, and let it out. Slowly, he smiled. Then without a word, he went on walking.

"Rocco! Didn't you hear?" she cried.

"I heard." He was still walking, and she followed, unsure of him, unsure anymore of anything.

At the post office Rocco went in, bought the stamps, and came out again. He licked the stamps, placed them carefully on the envelope, then handed the letter to Simone. She was looking flushed and bewildered, and slightly angry. She took the letter, and read the address.

"It's to Alex!" she said, smiling, surprised. "You've written to Alex!"

"And to my little cousin," he said.

"She's only seven months old, Rocco."

"Dad says he read to me, when I was that age. Anyway, it's a drawing. Something she'll like. Well, don't stand staring at it, Simone. Post it."

She shook her head. "You post it," she said impulsively, giving it back. "Maybe the things you post have special luck."

"Perhaps I should put a blessing on it," he murmured, half smiling.

"It wouldn't do any harm," she said. But she wasn't prepared for his kind of blessing.

He sat down cross-legged on the pavement, and placed the letter on the ground in front of him. The wind rolled small pieces of gravel across it, and tossed his dark hair. "Beloved Mother-Father God," he began, and Simone covered her face with her hands, laughing.

"You're crazy!" she cried, embarrassed. "Stop it! Just post it!"

"Beloved Mother-Father God," he said again, quietly, and with feeling. "Take this thing I do, and make it a loving act of Thine. Take this intent, and mold it to Your will. And lead

Your children in the way of peace. Amen."

Then he lifted the letter high, in both his hands. "In Your name, I do this thing," he said. Then he stood up, and posted the letter.

Simone watched, her lips curved, but her eyes unsure. "You worry me sometimes," she said softly. "You really do."

An old lady came up, stood next to Rocco, and delved a long time in her shopping bag, muttering. Rocco turned, about to walk away, when he suddenly put his hand to his chest, alarmed.

"What is it now?" asked Simone, fearing another performance.

Rocco took out the leather bag, weighing it in his hands. He squeezed it, and felt only shifting dust inside.

"It's gone," he said, and she couldn't tell whether he was terrified, or ecstatic. Suddenly, to her total embarrassment, he unzipped his jeans, and dropped them. In a panic of utter joy, he looked for the scars on his leg. "They're gone!" he yelled.

The old lady looked up, horrified. Simone walked off, disowning him, her shoulders shaking with laughter. Rocco shot the old lady a brilliant smile, and pulled up his jeans and zipped them. He ran after Simone.

"You're mad, you know that?" she murmured, looking sideways into his face, and trying not to laugh. "Totally, marvelously, mad."

"I'm fine," he said, smiling. "The whole world's fine. And the paths I walk be good, so good."

And he put his arm around her neck, and they went on walking home.

point ® **THRILLERS**

Read them and scream!

☐ MC44330-5	**The Accident** Diane Hoh	$2.95
☐ MC43115-3	**April Fools** Richie Tankersley Cusick	$2.95
☐ MC44236-8	**The Baby-sitter** R.L. Stine	$2.95
☐ MC44332-1	**The Baby-sitter II** R.L. Stine	$3.25
☐ MC43278-8	**Beach Party** R.L. Stine	$2.95
☐ MC43125-0	**Blind Date** R.L. Stine	$2.75
☐ MC43279-6	**The Boyfriend** R.L. Stine	$2.95
☐ MC44316-X	**The Cheerleader** Caroline B. Cooney	$2.95
☐ MC44884-6	**The Return of the Vampire** Caroline B. Cooney	$2.95
☐ MC43291-5	**Final Exam** A. Bates	$2.95
☐ MC41641-3	**The Fire** Caroline B. Cooney	$2.95
☐ MC43806-9	**The Fog** Caroline B. Cooney	$2.95
☐ MC43050-5	**Funhouse** Diane Hoh	$2.95
☐ MC44333-0	**The Girlfriend** R.L. Stine	$3.25
☐ MC44904-4	**The Invitation** Diane Hoh	$2.95
☐ MC43203-6	**The Lifeguard** Richie Tankersley Cusick	$2.75
☐ MC44582-0	**Mother's Helper** A. Bates	$2.95
☐ MC44768-8	**My Secret Admirer** Carol Ellis	$2.75
☐ MC44238-4	**Party Line** A. Bates	$2.95
☐ MC44237-6	**Prom Dress** Lael Littke	$2.95
☐ MC44941-9	**Sister Dearest** D.E. Athkins	$2.95
☐ MC43014-9	**Slumber Party** Christopher Pike	$2.75
☐ MC41640-5	**The Snow** Christopher Pike	$2.75
☐ MC43280-X	**The Snowman** R.L. Stine	$2.95
☐ MC43114-5	**Teacher's Pet** Richie Tankersley Cusick	$2.95
☐ MC43742-9	**Thirteen** Edited by Tonya Pines	$3.25
☐ MC44235-X	**Trick or Treat** Richie Tankersley Cusick	$2.95
☐ MC43139-0	**Twisted** R.L. Stine	$2.75
☐ MC44256-2	**Weekend** Christopher Pike	$2.95
☐ MC44916-8	**The Window** Carol Ellis	$2.95

Available wherever you buy books, or use this order form.

Scholastic Inc., P.O. Box 7502, 2931 East McCarty Street, Jefferson City, MO 65102

Please send me the books I have checked above. I am enclosing $——————————(please add $2.00 to cover shipping and handling). Send check or money order — no cash or C.O.D.s please.

Name ————————————————————————————————

Address————————————————————————————————

City————————————————State/Zip——————————

Please allow four to six weeks for delivery. Offer good in the U.S. only. Sorry, mail orders are not available to residents of Canada. Prices subject to change. PT591